WE COULD STAY HERE
ALL NIGHT

WE COULD STAY HERE ALL NIGHT

stories by

Debbie Howlett

Porcepic Books
an imprint of

Beach Holme Publishing
Vancouver

This book is published by Beach Holme Publishing, #226—2040
West 12th Ave., Vancouver, BC, V6J 2G2. This is a Porcepic Book.

We acknowledge the generous
assistance of The Canada Council
and the BC Ministry of Small Business, Tourism and Culture.

THE CANADA COUNCIL | LE CONSEIL DES ARTS
FOR THE ARTS | DU CANADA
SINCE 1957 | DEPUIS 1957

Editor: Joy Gugeler
Production and Design: Teresa Bubela

Cover Art: *Bedroom* (1987) by Mary Pratt. Oil on masonite.
121.9 cm x 88.2 cm. Used with permission of the artist.

Canadian Cataloguing in Publication Data

Howlett, Debbie, 1964-
  We could stay here all night

  (A Porcépic Book)
  ISBN 0-88878-393-0

  I. Title.
PS8565.O94W4 1999   C813'.54   C99-910306-7
PR9199.3.H683W4 1999

For Nora,
and for Anne.

Acknowledgements

I am indebted to the community of writers in the Creative Writing Department at the University of British Columbia where I first began writing some of the stories collected in *We Could Stay Here All Night*. In particular, for their generosity and friendship, I would like to thank Jerry Newman, George McWhirter, Bryan Wade, and especially Linda Svendson. For her insight and gentle editorial suggestions, I'd like to thank Joy Gugeler.

For faith and unwavering support, I'd like to thank my incredible family: my parents Michael and Ellen Howlett, Susan Howlett, Brian Howlett, Sandy Howlett, Ken Rockwood, Sandra MacKenzie, and Tom Routledge. For much talk about books and boys, and lovely long letters that have followed me all over the map, a big *merci* to my friend Martha Hillhouse. And finally, to Sam and Jake, my beautiful boys, and Joe, thank you.

I am grateful to the following publications, and their editors, in which some of these stories appeared in an earlier form: *The Malahat Review*, "Vermont"; *grain*, "We Could Stay Here All Night"; *The Antigonish Review*, "Communion" and "Lent"; *Prairie Fire,* "Love Line" and "The Comfort Zone"; *Seventeen*, "Undertow"; *Room of One's Own*, "Still in the Dark." "Vermont" was also printed in *Best Canadian Stories* (1990); "The Broom Closet" appeared in *Words We Call Home*. "The Comfort Zone" won the 1997 Western Magazine Award for Fiction.

Contents

How Do I Look?

On the other side of the door where I am waiting for them, with my swimsuit rolled up in a towel, I can hear the clink of ice cubes Dad will let melt into a pool, a sweet swirl of something I'll help myself to later, when we are home again.

"Hey Champ," he says to Mum who is in there with him. "You ready yet?" Then he swallows the rest of the cocktail he fixed for himself at dinner and sets it down on the night table next to the double bed they sometimes share.

"Tahdaah," Mum says, sliding open the bathroom door between their room and mine. "I'm ready now." The box springs creak.

"You're not even changed yet," he says in a flat tone of voice like he's not impressed.

"I'll change there," she tells him. "What's the matter with you tonight? I always change there." But he doesn't like waiting for her to slip into her bathing suit, or lock the back door, or double-check to make sure everything's unplugged— when he's ready, he just wants to go.

From where I am standing, listening with one ear pressed to the door, I hear him heave himself up off the bed. There is more creaking, this time across the floorboards which are old and wooden.

"Not now, Fred," Mum says, coughing. Her throat is choked with smoke. Quietly she tells him how in the kitchen my brother Wayne and his friend Frankie are chomping at the bit. "Those two aren't going to wait forever," she says. Then she opens the door and spies me standing there, ready and waiting to go too. "All set, Kipper," she says, smiling at me. Kipper is her name for me; Diane is his.

Mum steps down the staircase gracefully, with one hand trailing along the bannister, but I am awkward and noisy in my flip-flops clamouring after her. In the kitchen, Wayne and Frankie are firing spitballs at each other through bent drinking straws, the kind Dad can still drink through when he is flat on his back in bed. Frankie jumps up from behind the table, aims, then ducks back down quick. The spitball hits the fridge door, sticks there next to the hydro bill. Mum and I laugh at Frankie until Dad comes into the room carrying his empty glass. Then we keep quiet. He dumps the ice cubes into the sink.

He is reaching for a refill when a spitball hits him on the back of the head. In the silent kitchen one of the boys goes, "Hee hee."

"Jesus, Joseph, and Mary," he says. But before he can turn around to cuff someone, Mum says, "That's enough, boys," and scoots the two of them out the screen door and into the Impala where Granny is already tucked in the back seat out of Dad's way. I stay behind in the kitchen with him, watching as he splashes more gin into his glass. He chugs it down, then looks deep into the bottom of the glass. He eyes the Beefeater bottle sitting there on the counter with its label peeled off, then sees me.

"What are you waiting for Diane?" he says.

I hold open the screen door, inviting more flies inside to buzz around the sticky yellow tape that hangs in strips from the ceiling. "I'm waiting for you, Dad."

"You are?" he says, like I'm not the last one out the door every night.

I fold my arms across my chest. "Are you ready to go?"

"I'm burning to go," he finally says, whacking his chest with the end of one fist like he has to burp.

For Frankie's benefit, as we are backing out of the driveway, Dad tells us again how Mum taught Wayne to swim when he was just a baby. "Front crawl, back crawl, side stroke," he says, listing them off on his fingers as we wait for the light at the end of our street to turn green. "Did I forget any?" he asks us, but Mum says the question is rhetorical.

The light changes, but we stay idling at the white line until he remembers the breast stroke. "Breast stroke," he says. "I knew there was another one." Then he takes his foot off the clutch too quickly, and we all lurch forward into the intersection before sinking back into our seats again. Mum tightens her grip on the safety belt which she wears snugly buckled around her hips.

"I was a water rat, eh Dad?" asks Wayne.

"That's an understatement," he says. "You and your mother." Dad winks at Wayne in the rear view mirror, but from my spot in the front beside him I can see his pale eye snap shut, too. "Yes sir, your mother here just dropped you in the water wearing a pair of wings."

Beside me on the seat, Mum says, "I didn't drop him anywhere," before going back to staring out the car window on her side. Out the window, she looks at the maple trees until we reach the Seaway, the swimming pool at the end of the street. From there, we all stare at the city of Montreal squatting in a cloud of smog on the other side of the St. Lawrence River in the sweltering July heat. Mum tells us that it only took Wayne one week of flapping before he got the hang of it, and now he swims beautifully. "Like a fish," she says proudly.

My mother always says that my brother swims like a fish, but it is really Mum who is the swimmer in the family. She was the Quebec Junior Provincial Champion two years in a row, and won the Hardman trophy one year and the Gayle trophy the next for her synchronised swimming routines.

"You were the champ two years running, weren't you, Ruthie?" Dad asks her tonight. But she won't answer him when he is like this, all loud and full of hot air, so he starts talking about her like she isn't even here. "She had a synchronised swimming partner, too, before I came along. They were a pair."

From her cramped space in the back seat between Wayne and Frankie, Granny pipes up. "They were a duet, Fred, not a pair." Dad's shoulders go up, but instead of turning around like last night when he nearly plowed our car into the chain link fence that surrounds the pool, he keeps his eyes on the road in front of him like he's learned his lesson.

Oblivious to the faces he pulls up front in the mirror, Granny says what's on her mind. "Her partner's name was Olga and she and her weightlifter husband tried to defect to Canada. They hid out in my basement for two months until the oil man discovered them when he was reading the meter and squealed."

"Right," Dad snorts. "And now they live in Siberia where they are probably freezing in minus fifty degree temperatures."

Frankie says, "Where's Siberia, Mr. Wilkinson?"

But Mum says softly, "Up north."

Back in 1960 before I was born, Mum and Wayne used to practise kips and cranes and walkovers for hours at the Seaway in the summertime. "Some nights," Dad tells Frankie, "I'd have to drive down and get them after a twelve-hour shift, and by then Wayne'd be blue."

"He was hardly blue, Frankie," Mum says, exhaling.

"You were sculling before you were walking, Wayne," Dad calls over the seat. "You could pike and tuck and arch like a pro by the time you were eight months old."

"Wow," Frankie says, leaning forward. His face beams as he watches Mum light one Cameo off the butt of another, and sigh. Dad circles the gravel parking lot again, looking for just the right space. Last night after our near miss, we cruised around the lot for twenty minutes while Dad counted his lucky stars.

"Yoo hoo," says Dad, trying to get Mum's attention again. But she is still ignoring him, staring at the medal that dangles from his key ring. It is the Lieutenant Governor's medal she shared with Olga before she went into what my grandmother still refers to as "early retirement" in 1959—the year she got pregnant with Wayne. The medal is gold, and has her old name—Ruth Ellen Gallagher—stamped on it.

At home, we have a whole shelf in the family room with Mum's prizes on it, and then another box of prizes in the basement with both Mum's and Olga's name engraved on them. Mum looks at the ones on the shelf sometimes, when she is dusting over there and her cloth gets caught up on one of the little swimmers' legs, but avoids them the rest of the time. She never looks at what's in the basement.

"Then what happened?" Frankie asks Dad, but we all stay quiet as Dad shifts into neutral and cuts the engine. We know the rest of the story. Mum gave up synchro altogether in 1962, then she had me.

Only a few other families went to family swim as regularly as we did that summer. We all notice, keep tabs on who is coming and who is going. Sometimes on the way home, Mum and Dad talk about who was there and who wasn't, with Granny adding her two cents' worth from her seat in the back between Wayne and me. Wayne and I listen, but we don't say anything.

They take us swimming in the evenings when the sun isn't so high in the sky and hot. We have a family pass, but each little card has our own picture on it. The pictures are black and white and were taken in the Fotomat at the mall;

four poses for a dollar. Only Mum's picture is out of focus and doesn't look anything like her—her mouth is an O. She has this trick though, of keeping her thumb over her face whenever she has to show it to someone before quickly stuffing it away. The passes are good until the end of August and are for our family only.

This time though, we are bringing Frankie Lester along with us so Dad tells the man at the gate that Frankie is his long lost son come home again and slips him a buck. Wayne thinks it is all right, having Frankie as a brother, because he is tired of only having me to boss around all the time. But Mum says Wayne doesn't mean that, says he'd be sick of bossing Frankie in no time flat.

Mum and I change into our bathing suits in one room and Dad and the boys change in another. Mum wears a one-piece, with a racing stripe down the side of it. She calls this suit her swimming suit. My suit is a two-piece, but it is not a bikini. Dad says I am too young for a bikini, but Mum says she had one when she was five, and "We'll see, Kipper."

"Aren't you a skinny mini," Mum says as she tugs the top piece over my head. Then she smoothes her palm over my bare stomach and smiles. After we have our suits on, Mum walks on tiptoes over to the mirror and starts tucking her long straight hair into her bathing cap. Her cap is from the old days, and has rcd sequins sewn on it.

It doesn't take the boys as long as it takes us, and by the time Mum and I are done, Wayne and Frankie are wet and soaking Dad in the shallow end of the pool. Dad pretends to mind, but doesn't really.

When Dad sees us, he puts his thumb and his finger in his mouth and whistles. He whistles loud and shrill enough for everyone to hear; even Granny hears and looks up from her Harlequin romance.

The lifeguard looks over to where Dad is standing, waist-deep, to see what all the commotion is about. Mum gives him a look that says she is embarrassed he did that, but he reaches out to us as we shuffle past. He closes a big hand around Mum's ankle and she is trapped, but I run up ahead. "You're a bathing beauty in that cap, Champ," he says, then lets her go.

Wayne does a handstand in the water and says, "Watch this one, Dad." Dad watches Wayne, but he watches Mum, too, as she walks away from him to where Granny sits keeping the cigarettes and the towels dry.

"Come on, girls," Dad calls. He makes a megaphone out of one hand that carries his voice across the water to where we are stalling. Mum and I like taking our time getting wet. We inch our way in, toe by toe, and no one is allowed to splash us until we are all the way in.

"Last one in is a rotten egg," Wayne says in a singsong, but Mum is quick to say, "Never mind that," looking at me.

I am usually all wet and jumping around before Mum is in anyway.

Before dark, Dad wants to take me into the deep end with him, but Mum thinks I am too little. "Leave her be, Fred," Mum says to him. But he wants to take me for a ride on his back, and I want to go. I don't know how to swim yet (I am still a beginner) so Mum says slowly, "Hang onto him tight and don't let go, okay?" I have my hands clasped around Dad's neck as he begins to move us away from everyone.

Wayne and Frankie stay in the shallow end with Mum. "Someone has to keep an eye on them," Mum says. Then she says to Dad, "You be careful."

"You worry too much," he says. His deep voice makes his throat vibrate, my hands shiver.

Mum sucks hard on her bottom lip. She always sucks hard on her bottom lip when she is nervous about something; that, or she smokes too many cigarettes. But there is "No Smoking" at the swimming pool during family swim, only later, on the way home.

When Dad and I reach the deep end he says, "You're getting heavy," but I tell him what Mum always says—"I'm light as air, I'm a feather."

"Maybe we'll sink to the bottom if you don't start kicking your legs soon, Feather," he says, kidding. I can kick my legs, they showed us kicking in beginner class, so I kick them up behind me, making a big splash.

"That's better," he says. "You're getting it now."

We tour around the whole of the deep end with Dad making little chugging sounds the entire time. We swim in the shade of the diving boards where the water temperature is cooler than it is in other places, and around the ropes. I wave at the lifeguard, but the lifeguard doesn't wave back. Dad says she is too busy watching the clock and waiting to go home.

I count three diving boards in this end of the pool, two

lower ones, and then a higher board that makes a nice twangy sound whenever someone uses it.

"Look, there's Wayne," Dad says, taking his hand out of the water and pointing. I bob up.

Wayne and Frankie stand in a line to use the lower boards, but Wayne's diving isn't very good. Most of his dives wind up as belly flops with Wayne's stomach smacking the water like the sound of Dad's hand. Frankie is better, and his mum wasn't even a champ or anything.

They do cannonballs mostly, and can openers, and pin-drops, and a few hi-karates, with all of the families cheering and clapping and paying attention while Wayne and Frankie ham it up. Granny pays attention, too, while Dad and I watch from the side of the pool, holding on.

Back in the old days, before I was born, Granny used to watch Mum swim too. She says that she knew some of Mum's routines even better than Mum did, but Mum says in all that time, Granny never once got her feet wet. Wayne and I think swimming is something grannies just don't do.

In the deep end, Dad makes wide circles with his arms and his legs and calls it treading water. "The water is almost ten feet deep here," he says.

I say, "That's deep."

"Is it ever."

We start swimming again, then Dad says, "Let's head back. I need a break." But I don't want to head back to Wayne and Frankie hamming it up and Mum just standing there worrying. I want to stay in this end of the pool where the water is cool and mysterious and ten feet deep.

"No, let's stay here," I say, pleading with him, but he decides to take me back to the shallow end and Mum. And when we get there, he has to pull my hands from around his neck.

"I'll just do a few lengths, Diane," he says to me. "What's wrong with you anyway?" Then he says to Mum, "Back before you know it. I'll just cross the deep end a few times."

Mum nods and watches him going off across the pool, slapping the water, all arms and legs. When Dad is gone, Mum tries to cheer me up by putting her hands under the small of my back and helping me to float, but I say, "Don't, Mum," and push her away. Then I look into the deep end for Dad.

In a quiet voice Mum calls Wayne and Frankie over to where the two of us are standing. Then she asks us if we want to see one of her routines. She goes, "Sshhh," because she wants it to be our secret.

Wayne goes, "But there isn't any music, Mum." But Mum says that's okay, she'll listen to the music that is in her head.

It is a long routine. Mum disappears below the surface of the water and spins around like an upside-down figure skater. She shoots one leg out of the water, and holds it, turning, calls it a flamingo. When she reappears, Mum takes what she says is a sip of air because your audience isn't supposed to see you gasping for it, then she heads back across the water, cutting it with long smooth strokes. She makes small whirlpools with her legs, and sends her body bobbing up for air before slipping under again, somersaulting, spinning into a corkscrew. This time, Wayne and Frankie and I hold our breath, too.

"Mum?" I whisper. But she is underwater for two or three minutes maybe.

At the end, she duck dives deep into the water and comes springing out with her arms stretched into a big V. Her signature move, she tells us, the big finish that everyone will always remember her for.

Wayne and Frankie Lester and I applaud like crazy, but breathing hard, Mum says she isn't nearly as graceful as she used to be on account of the pin. Mum has a steel pin in her calf from a car accident they had and it weighs her down. It isn't supposed to, the doctors say she should be weightless under the water, but Mum says she can feel it pulling her under the minute she starts anything down there, and that is final.

We think her routine is graceful anyway. But she says, "You're just saying that, you three," and doesn't believe us. She goes from looking at me to looking at Wayne to looking at Granny.

By the time Dad comes back from his swim, I am covered in goose bumps and Mum has me in her arms. She lifts me out of the water.

"Don't catch cold," she says as I run over to Granny. "Use my towel too."

Mum stays in the water with the others while I snuggle

up next to Granny. "Did you see that, Granny?" I ask her and Granny says that yes, she saw it.

Usually during family swim, Mum doesn't do very much swimming at all. She crawls across the pool once or twice holding her head out of the water, and scissors kicks her legs behind her. But tonight she is out of breath from swimming so hard, and her hair hangs out in long wet strands from under her cap.

"Jesus Christ," Dad says to her. "Did you fall in? You're soaking wet." He twists a strand of her hair around his finger and tugs it. "It's a bloody shame, you know," he tells her.

But, "You don't know anything about a bloody shame," is all Mum says to him. Then she leans against the side of the pool with her arms held out and her palms touching the cement. Dad slaps the water with his hand and sends a wave in Mum's direction. Then he scoops Wayne up in his arms and dunks him with a one, two, three. Wayne sails a little ways through the air before hitting the water with a slap and going under.

"My turn next," says Frankie, so Dad sends Frankie flying too. They are still at it when Mum and I sneak away with towels tucked around our waists and our teeth chattering.

In the changing room Mum steps out of her wet suit and back into her sundress. She gets me to zip her up, then she turns around. "How do I look?"

I watch Mum's face, but she doesn't give anything away. She just stands there with her hands useless by her sides, waiting for an answer. I say, "Mum, your face's wet."

She smiles at me, then she crouches down low so we can

see each other eye-to-eye. She tells me that Olga and Dmitri are a real love story, the kind you only read about in romance books and some nights it makes her sad to think about them, that's all.

After family swim Dad always takes us somewhere special for treats like Pepsis and Maywests or Nutty Buddies and Space Bars. Some nights the treats are almost as good as the swimming. Where we go is always a big surprise though, even Mum doesn't know.

Tonight they are all hushed up and standing in a clump when Mum and I come out of the changing rooms.

Dad says to us, "Get in the car," so the three of us pile into the seats in a hurry, beating Granny, and burn the backs of our legs on the still-hot vinyl.

Once we are all in the car and waiting, Mum breaks the silence and says, "Where are we going, Dad?"

Love Line

Our dad's brother is Lenny Wilkinson and he lives in the United States of America. We don't see him very often, once every five years, but he turned up that August with a woman named Laura. Uncle Lenny says that Laura is his new wife. Then he pats her on the bum, right in front of my brother and me.

"Wife, eh?" Mum says to Dad, under her breath.

Dad says, "Now Ruth," but you can tell he doesn't believe it either.

Dad and Uncle Lenny shake hands like strangers. "I told Laura you'd read her palm," Uncle Lenny says, first thing.

My father likes to read our neighbours' palms after church on Sundays when he isn't working on boilers. He met our mother that way, the year the Canadian Nationals landed her in an Olympic-sized swimming pool on the outskirts of Montreal. He swam into her lane during a free swim and sent her duck-diving deep to avoid him. Mum was still swimming synchro then, representing her country in the singles competition and travelling from meet to meet with Granny, her chaperone and coach.

Soaking wet and shivering all over, Dad traced her love line with a finger and told her it was like looking into a mirror. "I'm here," he told her. "And here and here and here." Mum married him in July that same year, in the parish of St. Ignatius, in the middle of a heat wave, because she loved him and she was going to have his baby and it was 1959.

Laura holds out her hand to Dad, but he just shakes it instead. "There'll be plenty of time for palm reading," Dad says to her.

Uncle Lenny owns a company called Hocus Pocus in the state of Nevada. The company supplies magicians with what Uncle Lenny calls "tricks of the trade."

Uncle Lenny is just in town for a few days and needs a place to stay. "What do you say, Freddy?" Uncle Lenny says to Dad. Mum and Dad and Uncle Lenny are getting reacquainted again in Uncle Lenny's car while Wayne and Laura and I are sitting on the front stoop. Wayne tells us that Mum and Uncle Lenny and Dad used to be friends, but they're not friends anymore.

Laura says, "Why not?"

Wayne shrugs his shoulders and says he was too young to remember.

Mum raises her voice and I hear her say something about "that funny business." Then she says, "How long are you staying?" She is smoking in the back seat of Uncle Lenny's Rambler, listening to him and leaning forward on her elbows. The engine is humming, but the car isn't going anywhere. It has been places though and to prove it, Uncle Lenny has plastered the bumper with stickers from as far away as Fort Lauderdale and British Columbia and Lake Tahoe.

"Just a couple of days," Uncle Lenny says. He opens the car door and steps out into the bright yellow sunlight. "You two think about it," he says. He shuts the car door, tight. Then he takes three giant steps towards us. Beside me, Laura yawns. She and Uncle Lenny drove all night to get here.

Mum flicks her cigarette out the car window and it lands on the hot pavement next to the one she flicked out a few minutes ago.

"Can you take us around the block, Fred?" she asks, buckling up. She wants to mull things over. Dad slides over into the driver's seat. He places his hands at ten and two on the steering wheel, then slips the car into reverse. As he backs down the driveway, he stares out the windshield at me and Wayne. I wave.

Dad and Uncle Lenny have a reunion in the basement of our house with a couple of six packs of Molson Canadian while Laura takes a catnap in my room. Mum says it reminds her of the old days.

"What old days?" I ask her. We are in the kitchen listening to Dad and Uncle Lenny ham it up downstairs. I am timing soft boiled eggs to earn my cooking badge for Brownies and Wayne is eating them.

Back then, Mum says Uncle Lenny made his living renting

out tables at the Magic City Pool Room. She says that she and Dad and Lenny used to do stuff together when Lenny lived in the city still. Wayne wants to know what kind of "stuff."

"Parties, dances, that kind of stuff," she says.

"Dad used to dance?" asks Wayne. We've seen Mum dance with Father Paul and Mr. Lester and everyone at the St. Patrick's Day dance every year, but we've never seen her dance with Dad.

Mum says softly, "Your father watched."

The buzzer on the timer goes, and I fish the egg out of the water with a spoon. It has a crack in it already, and long white tentacles reach out from under the shell.

Wayne says the last one was runny.

Mum and I watch as Wayne slices off the top half of the egg. It comes off like a hat.

Wayne says, "So far so good."

Mum makes a joke and calls Wayne "an egg-spert." We all laugh until we hear a little crash downstairs that wakes Laura up and sends Mum flying. Wayne and I follow Mum, with straight faces. Uncle Lenny is on the floor, holding his sides because something's very funny. Dad is there, too, laughing and carrying on with a can of beer in his hand. They broke a lamp. Mum's favourite.

Before dinner, Mum sews on the little brown patch with the golden pot on it, even though my third attempt at the egg wound up hard-boiled. She puts it next to the one I got for thriftiness. Laura sits next to Mum, leaning back on her chair. She is brushing out her hair, which is still wet from the Mr. Bubble bath she took. She's using my squirrel comb.

"What's this one for?" she asks me. She points at a badge with a broom on it. She thinks my uniform is cute.

"Housekeeping," I say. Then I tell Laura how it took me a week of sweeping and vacuuming to get the badge. "It was the toughest one," I say. "I had to clean the whole house."

"Howse," she says, imitating me. She has an American accent that Mum says sounds crass and stupid. Laura thinks we sound British.

Mum and Laura don't exactly hit it off. Mum says that Laura is tacky. She tells Dad that Uncle Lenny could have done better.

"Better?" Dad says, only half-listening to her.

"Much better," she says, then storms around the house fuming silently.

I like Laura. She is very pretty, and she has a nice laugh that echoes through the house. She laughs a lot, especially around Dad, who she thinks is a scream.

Mum says, "He's a laugh, all right."

Dad raids the linen cupboard for a towel he can wrap around his head like a turban, then comes into the kitchen.

"What do you think?" he says to Mum.

Mum says, "Not much," without looking up from her sewing. She is still mad about that lamp. Laura roars.

I say, "I like it."

The turban is Uncle Lenny's idea. "Everyone does this stuff in Reno," Dad says.

"This isn't Reno," Mum says.

Uncle Lenny comes into the room with another can of beer. He blows a kiss in Laura's direction and Laura pretends to catch it in the palm of her hand. She presses her palm up to her mouth.

"Johnny Carson does this turban stuff on "The Tonight Show," Uncle Lenny tells us. He tucks a piece of the towel behind Dad's ear so it's tight. "It kills 'em."

Wayne says, "Who's Johnny Carson?"

"Haven't you ever seen "The Tonight Show?" asks Uncle Lenny.

Wayne and I shake our heads, staring at Dad. We are the only house on our block with an outdoor aerial, and Mum says it is an eyesore. The aerial picks up three crumby channels in good weather, two in rain. It is finicky. On Saturdays, Dad hogs the changer and sends our aerial spinning out of control, while Wayne and I fetch cigarettes and beer from the *dépanneur* on the corner. From a distance our house always looks as if it is preparing for flight. We can hear the whirring of the antenna two blocks away.

On the way back Wayne always says, "Ahem, pilot to co-pilot, pilot to co-pilot." He speaks into his clenched fist and clears his throat.

I am the stewardess, offering "Beer, cigarettes?" to the passengers, or sometimes I am the co-pilot. It doesn't matter, the game always ends the same way. During takeoff, the house, with Dad in the cockpit, careens off course and slams into the St. Lawrence River.

The rest of the houses on the block are connected by

underground lines, and they get cable TV. Even the Lesters get cable TV. We get two English stations and one lousy French one.

"What you kids are missing," Uncle Lenny says, whistling through his teeth. "Believe you me."

Uncle Lenny tells me and Wayne that Johnny Carson is a late night talk show host who is better than Ed Sullivan. Mum says to Uncle Lenny that no one's better than Ed, then she tells Dad that he looks silly.

In the basement, Uncle Lenny and Laura put on a magic show. Uncle Lenny is the magician and Laura is his assistant. "What do you want me to do, Lenny?" Laura says, but he doesn't give her anything specific to do, so she just stands around wearing a fancy sequined hat, waving her arms every once in a while and sending feathers sailing in all directions.

Before the show, Dad and Uncle Lenny carted boxes from the trunk of his car into our house. "This stuff is great," Dad told Uncle Lenny. He poked at the stuff in the boxes, until Mum came down the stairs. Then he took his place in the audience beside her.

The first thing Uncle Lenny does is make a Canadian dollar disappear.

"How did you do that, Uncle Lenny?" Wayne wants to know.

Uncle Lenny says, "Easy," but when he looks up his shirt sleeve it is empty. "Where the hell did it go?" he says. Wayne and I help him look for the bill, but we don't find it. Dad says it'll turn up sooner or later.

For his next trick, Uncle Lenny cuts a deck of cards in half and gets Wayne to pick a card. Wayne shows it to me and Mum, but not to Uncle Lenny. It is the four of spades. Wayne gives Uncle Lenny back the card and Uncle Lenny cuts the deck again. Laura gives it a tap. Then Uncle Lenny holds his hand up to his forehead for a moment and closes his eyes.
"Is this your card?" he says, showing us the palm of his hand with the four of spades lying face up.

We want to know how he does that one, too. He says, "That one is simple." He knows which card Wayne will choose by the way he cuts the deck, then he puts a dab of Krazy glue in the palm of his hand, so when he gets the card back, it sticks.

Next Uncle Lenny pulls an egg out of my ear.

"Neat," I say. Wayne and Dad and I clap while Uncle Lenny takes a bow, but Mum says she's seen it all before.

Uncle Lenny is Dad's younger brother, but Dad hadn't laid eyes on him in over five years the day he turned up in the Rambler. During dinner, Dad asks Uncle Lenny what he's doing so far from home. He says, "I'm travelling."

"Travelling where, Len?" Mum says. She looks at him across the table. Wayne says she hasn't warmed up to him yet.

"Around," Uncle Lenny says, with a mouthful of food. Then he says to her, "Mmmmm." We are eating lamb chops, even though it is only Wednesday, because Uncle Lenny and

Laura are here. We are even having wine with dinner, a bubbly with a picture of a duck on the label. According to Uncle Lenny, it is one of Laura's favourites.

"Must be nice," Dad says, meaning travelling. Then Uncle Lenny says he has an idea for a syndicated TV magic show he is sure he could sell to the CBC.

Dad says, "A magic show, eh?"

"I'm still only thinking," Uncle Lenny says.

"Good luck," Mum says. "Times are tough."

Uncle Lenny looks at Dad. "Is that something you might be interested in, Freddy?"

From where I'm sitting between Laura and my brother, I know Dad's considering it.

"You'd get to be the star of the show, of course," Uncle Lenny says. "You could predict the future, say, by looking into a crystal ball."

Dad looks at his palms. "The future, eh?"

"It's a safe bet." Uncle Lenny tells us he knows all about safe bets, odds-making. He's chummy with blackjack dealers and keno runners, but swears on a stack of Holy Bibles that he himself never gambles on anything but a sure thing.

Uncle Lenny helps himself to another chop and splashes it with mint sauce. He says there's money in magic.

Mum wants to know how much money he is talking about.

"Piles," he says. For the rest of the meal, we chew without talking.

After Mum and I clear away the dinner plates, Uncle Lenny hands me two American quarters and winks. The quarters are dirty. Then he asks me if my brother and I wouldn't be happier out in the front yard where it is still sunny and hot. I look over at Mum, who nods at me.

Wayne and I take our dirty quarters outside and sweat in the paved lot Uncle Lenny has called our "yard." Earlier that summer, Dad had concrete poured over our front lawn because he was tired of mowing it. In the still wet cement, my brother and I flattened out our palms. Tonight we take turns tossing our quarters into the hand prints while inside the house Uncle Lenny gives Mum and Dad the "hard sell." He wants Dad to invest in his magic company so the company can keep the TV show well-supplied with two-headed coins, whoopie cushions, false-bottomed closets, you name it. Passing by the open window, I hear Uncle Lenny call it "up front money."

Wayne says in the five years that Uncle Lenny has been out of the city of Montreal, he has been around the world, maybe more than once.

"How do you know?" I say. Wayne says that Uncle Lenny told him so.

"Look here," Wayne says, digging in a pocket. He pulls out some matchbooks that Uncle Lenny gave him from a night-club in Las Vegas, Nevada. The matchbooks have pictures of women on them, bare naked. Wayne shows them to me, but he's not supposed to show them to Mum. On the inside cover, the ladies have printed in their names and phone numbers, real neat.

"This is Cleo," Wayne says, showing off. Cleo has blonde hair to her waist, and a nice set of teeth. "Kitty," Wayne says next. Kitty is brunette, and from the neck up she looks like Mum, only friendlier. Wayne holds up another matchbook and says, "This one's name is Candy. Uncle Lenny says she's long-distance, but worth the nickel."

For a married man, I say Uncle Lenny sure has a lot of girlfriends. "Eh Wayne?" I say.

Wayne says, "He sure does." Then he says that Laura looks a lot like the matchbook women. We pore over the matchbooks until Mum yells out the window that it's time for Brownies.

Uncle Lenny offers to give me a lift to Brownies, while Mum and Dad stay home to argue about the TV magic show. Dad wants to invest in Uncle Lenny's show, but Mum says no. Wayne says what she says goes.

In the church parking lot, Uncle Lenny spots Tawny Owl climbing out of her little Volkswagen, and says, "Who's that, Diane?"

"That's just Tawny Owl," I say. Tawny Owl became our pack leader last month when Brown Owl quit in a huff.

"Hold on," says Uncle Lenny. He steers his car into the slot beside the statue of the Virgin and tells me he's coming in too. I remind him that there are no boys in Brownies, but he says he doesn't mind. He says he thinks he'll like being the only boy in the troop.

"We're a pack," I say.

Our Brownie pack meets every Wednesday night in the church basement, rain or shine. On the way in, Uncle Lenny says, "Christ, I haven't been in a Catholic church in years."

I ask him, "What about when you got married?"

He looks my way, but doesn't say anything. Then he mumbles something about how he and Laura got married quickly in a little chapel off the strip in Sin City. "Nothing fancy, Diane," he says.

Uncle Lenny wants to stay with me at Brownies because he thinks it looks like fun. I ask Tawny Owl. She says okay, Uncle Lenny can stay.

"Thanks, Tawny," Uncle Lenny says, then he tells her he knew a nice girl named Tawny once.

"Is that right?" Tawny Owl says, smiling. Then she whispers to him that Tawny Owl isn't her real name.

"It ought to be," he whispers back. "It suits you."

When Uncle Lenny and Tawny Owl finish whispering, she invites him to sit in the Brownie ring, next to her; we all hold hands. I am across the room from them, between Patty and a Tweenie. I show Patty my cooking badge, but I don't let the Tweenie see it. The Tweenie is a French girl who isn't even a Brownie, but tonight's her big night.

Tawny Owl gives Uncle Lenny a big Brownie welcome, and makes him take the pledge with us. Then we all sing and dance around the toadstool. We sing, "We're the Brownies, here's our aim, lend a hand and play the game." Uncle Lenny sings, too, even though he doesn't know the words.

Afterwards, we break into smaller powwows to think up good deeds. Uncle Lenny stays beside Tawny Owl and helps her set up the enchanted forest on the other side of the basement. When they are finished, Uncle Lenny asks all the

Brownies to form a circle again. His voice is high-pitched. We take our places while Uncle Lenny hands out flashlights. Then he switches off the lights.

During the Tweenie ceremony, we wave our flashlights around the room like fairy lights. I shine mine in the direction of Uncle Lenny and catch him whispering something to Tawny Owl that makes her giggle and look away.

Once the Tweenies have walked through the enchanted forest, Uncle Lenny turns on the lights again. Tawny Owl calls him her little helper.

"There's magic in love," Tawny Owl says to the Tweenies. "Use it every day in all you do, and see what wonderful things happen to you."

"A-men," says Uncle Lenny. At the end of the ceremony, Tawny Owl taps the Tweenies on the head and turns them into Brownies, while Uncle Lenny teaches them the Brownie handshake.

Patty's mother drives me home, after Uncle Lenny volunteers to stay and help Tawny Owl clean up the crêpe paper river and the stepping stones.

"This could take all night," Uncle Lenny says to me.

When I get home, Dad is reading Laura's hand in the living room. He has taken off the turban and the two of them are having drinks on ice.

"Uh huh," Dad is saying.

"Is something wrong?" Laura says. She tries to pull her hand away, but Dad hangs on to it.

"Look at that love line," he says. I am standing in the doorway. I cough. Dad looks up. He says, "Look at this,

Diane." He drags his finger across her palm and asks me if I have ever seen anything like it. I shake my head, no. Laura's love line cuts her palm in two.

"Want to watch me read Laura's palm?" Dad asks me.

I say, "No thanks," and head upstairs. In my room, I practise tying and untying the reef knot in my scarf until Mum comes in.

"Where's Lenny?" asks Mum. Her cheeks are flushed.

"I don't know," I tell her. I don't tell her that Uncle Lenny stayed for Brownies, though I don't know why not.

She tells me to get into bed, then after a few minutes, she calls, "Lights out." I turn off the lamp beside my bed, but I don't fall asleep; I am too wound up. I am thinking about the magic show and Uncle Lenny and Mum and Dad and Laura and I am trying to piece it all together.

They're all in the kitchen the next morning when I get up: Mum, Dad, Wayne, Uncle Lenny and Laura. Laura is wearing Mum's good car coat over something strapless and Uncle Lenny is in the light blue seersucker suit he drove up in. I wave at Dad, but he is too wrapped up in something Mum is saying to him a few inches in front of his face.

When the telephone rings, they all stop talking and look at me. I get the phone. It is Tawny Owl. She says, "Good morning, Diane." Then she says she needs to talk to Lenny. I turn around and hold the receiver out for Uncle Lenny.

"Uncle Lenny," I say. "It's Tawny."

Mum says, "Give me that." She takes the receiver from

my hand, grabs it really, and then gives Tawny Owl a piece of her mind. When she hangs up, they go back to arguing about the magic business, and about that other business Mum calls the funny business.

Uncle Lenny says, "Ruth, we're all family."

Mum goes, "Some family," pointing at Laura.

Everyone is quiet after that, and Dad says he thinks Uncle Lenny and Laura ought to be on their way now because it is getting late.

Wayne and I hug Uncle Lenny and Laura out front, but Mum and Dad don't. Uncle Lenny tells Wayne and me that in the United States, they have thirty channels to choose from. "Or more," he says.

Uncle Lenny and Laura drive in a straight line away from us. They reach the end of our block before Mum realizes that Laura has gone with her good coat, the one she wears to church.

"Damn," she says, "I loved that coat." Then she says, "It's all your fault," looking at Dad.

Dad tells her he'll get her another one. But she's not buying it. She calls Laura a little tramp.

When Uncle Lenny's car is almost out of sight, Dad starts back toward the house and Wayne and I follow him. Mum stays where she is, watching her coat disappear, until it is just a memory of a thing she once loved.

Communion

We're all in church on Sunday—Mum and Wayne and me on the one side of the aisle, Granny in her favourite spot on the other side—when Dad comes in during the Consecration and takes a seat in the pew beside Mum. Mum looks at him for a moment, then at his beard, then back into her missal. She gestures for me and Wayne to do the same thing.

"Amen," we say and Wayne nudges me with his elbow to make sure I've recognized Dad. But I have. The whole congregation has.

This morning we sing verses of "Silent Night" in English and Latin during the Offertory. Since the start of Advent, Father Paul has been gearing up for the holidays—slipping in a Christmassy hymn or two during the quieter parts, wearing fancier robes. This one is maroon-coloured with gold braids down the front and back of it. Someday I'd like to wear gold braids like Father Paul's, but Mum's always saying things like "Dream On" and "Not in this lifetime."

Dad's voice booms above our three voices. He croons

"'Round young virgin mother and child," as Mum gives quarters out of her purse to Wayne and me to chuck into the basket when it comes by. This is usually our favourite part, but this Sunday we are almost too intent, too interested in watching what happens between the two of them when Miss Penny comes by with the collection basket. Miss Penny taps Wayne on the shoulder to get his attention, so he stops scowling at Dad.

"Hey look, it's Miss Penny," Wayne says and waves. Mum goes "Sshhh," but looks directly at Miss Penny without smiling as she slips her envelope into the basket. Then she looks back at Dad, but she isn't smiling at him anymore either. Wayne and I watch Miss Penny disappear up the aisle with the basket. Last week after Mass, Mum told us that letting ladies take up Collection was a big deal and about time. She said it was called liberation.

Anyway, Miss Penny used to teach the grade three-ers at our school, but now we don't see her very much because she's at another school. She was transferred because she got too involved. Wayne had her, but I didn't, and said she was all right.

During the Peace Offering, Dad shoots his arm around Mum's waist and pulls her close. She looks at him with an expression on her face that says she's embarrassed he's doing that, but he keeps it there anyway. And he even kisses her right on the lips in church and she smiles, so I smile and show a lot of teeth. He blows a kiss at me because I'm the furthest away and tries to run his hand through Wayne's hair before Wayne notices him doing that and pulls away. Then

Dad turns around and shakes hands with the Lesters. Mrs. Lester is tight-lipped but polite. Mr. Lester says, "Merry Christmas, Fred," even though Christmas is still a week away. Then Dad crosses the aisle and goes over to where Granny's sitting with her friends and squeezes her. As he crosses back he slips in a puddle of melted snow, but manages to steady himself before falling down hard on the marble floor.

The four of us go up for Communion together like old times—Dad in front and Mum behind—and they're careful to close up the space between us quickly and make room for everyone else in the aisle. Wayne doesn't want to be standing next to Dad, so he steps out of the line and into the aisle and tells me to go first. When I don't move, he gives me a little shove and tells me to get going. I look at Mum before moving up behind Dad, and she gives me her sad eyes. I hear her go, "Now, Wayne," but she doesn't sound mad.

Dad says, "Amen" to Father Paul and takes his on his tongue while the rest of us take it in our hands. I pop mine in right away without looking up at Father Paul, but Wayne's still got his in his hands when we get back to our seats. He knows he's not supposed to, but he plays with it a little while before shoving it into his mouth, turning it over in his palms and snapping it in half, until Dad sees him and tells him to smarten up or else. Dad shows Wayne the back of his hand and when Dad's not looking anymore, Wayne sticks out his tongue at him.

Coming out of church, Mum and Dad link arms and Wayne elbows me again. Mum's hand dips into the holy water and she makes a little splash as if the water's too cold

Debbie Howlett

and Dad makes a big show out of genuflecting in front of the crucifix. He keeps his head bent low the whole time he's down there on his knee and sweeps his arm way out in front of his body before standing up again. Wayne says something about penance that I don't catch and rolls his eyes. Then he says, "It won't last," and heads out the door.

Granny catches up with us in the back porch of the church and wants me and Wayne to go home with her for Cokes and hotdogs with mustard, but Mum says, "No, they'll stay with me." Dad goes out into the cold to get the car while Granny and Mum look at each other without saying anything. A frosty wind blows into the porch and makes Mum's eyes water. She dabs at them with her glove turned inside-out and Wayne and I stamp our feet to keep them warm. While we were inside praying, ice formed on the windshield so Dad has to get out of the car and scrape it off with the scraper Mum bought at Canadian Tire so we can see our way home.

But we don't go straight home. We stop at the Garden Bar-B-Q for lunch instead. Wayne makes a clucking noise with his tongue when he sees the neon chicken standing out in front and we all laugh; even Wayne laughs. We fill the car up with our laughter until the windows get all steamy and Dad has to crack his open to let some air in.

Because today is special, Wayne and I get to order our own chicken-in-a-basket instead of having to share one like usual. Each chicken comes in its own little red basket with a small pot of coleslaw, two containers of mayonnaise and packets of salt and pepper. It is the size of the things we like best and we eat mostly French fries dipped in mayonnaise and the pot of coleslaw. Mum drinks coffee and Dad says, "Only one" to her, before ordering a Blue and a glass of tomato juice. Mum says, "Don't start, Fred." Dad drinks half the can of beer and then pours the tomato juice right into the can and drinks the rest. He slurps up the tomato juice that gets trapped on the lip of the can and eats what Wayne and I leave behind in our baskets.

The waitress recognizes us from church.

Dad is extravagant, waves fifty dollar bills around. Mum looks the way she does when she's walking up the icy path to the house in her church shoes. She smokes too many cigarettes during lunch and the waitress has to empty the ashtray twice.

"What do you want for Christmas, Diane?" Dad wants to know. "A new Barbie doll?" I shake my head, no. At some point during the past year, my best friend in the whole entire world (Patty Templeton) and I have decided we are too old for Barbies. I want a china tea set instead.

"The tea game is very popular these days," Mum tells him. I remind her tea is not a game.

"What about you, Wayne? You want a tea set, too?" he asks.

Wayne screws up his face and says, "No way." He tells us he wants a new hockey stick. "A top-of-the-line stick," Wayne says. "Something that won't break by March this time."

Then he asks Mum what she wants, but she doesn't answer him.

On our way back from the restaurant, a cat runs into the street and Dad has to slam his foot on the brake so he doesn't run it over. I tell Dad to look out for the cat, but the car skids through a stop sign and another car almost hits us. Mum says, "Jesus, Joseph, and Mary" out loud and then, "Are you trying to kill us, Fred?" Dad doesn't say anything so she is quiet the rest of the way. Wayne bites into his bottom lip and makes it bleed, but he doesn't cry or complain. He just sits there looking out the window at the snow on the trees and sucks on his lip.

By Tuesday Dad's no longer sleeping on the couch and the dog comes looking for somewhere else to sleep after getting kicked out of Mum's bed. I take this as a good sign, though I'm not too sure what it means exactly. Wayne tells me not to count my chickens before they hatch. Wayne says he remembers Dad coming and going before, but I don't. And when we come home from school, Mum's there with Christmas cookies in the shape of Santa's reindeer and tall glasses of milk for us, and she moves about the house singing "God Rest Ye Merry Gentlemen" in a deep, funny voice. Dad is there, too, in his parka decorating the front of the house with red and green lights, Scotch taping Christmas cards to the bannister and hanging up fake mistle-toe in the doorways. I run through the doorways so as not to get caught by either of them, but sometimes let them catch me on purpose. A lot of kissing goes on in the house that week and I can't help but get caught up in it. Wayne is there the whole time though, reminding me not to get too excited.

Because school has let out for the holidays, we get to

hang around the house with the two of them during the day time. Mum smiles and says we're in her way and underfoot. Still, we get to go on lots of errands with Dad to give Mum some breathing room, like to the liquor store for what Dad calls libations for the big party, and to the Christmas tree lot behind the church. Dad tells the man in the Santa suit (Father Paul in a too-tight red suit and cotton batting glued to his face) he wants a special tree, something expensive and takes out the fifty dollar bills again. So Santa (Father Paul) takes Dad to the furthermost corner of the parking lot to look for special trees. Wayne goes with them, but I don't. Wayne concentrates on throwing snowballs up in the air and trying to catch them in his mittens before they break apart. Sometimes, his aim is off and the snowballs land on Dad. Wayne's careful not to hit Father Paul though.

I just stand there watching an entire family pile into a station wagon with a tree strapped on top when Miss Penny sneaks up behind me and says, "Hello, Diane," like she knows me. She looks way too dressed up to be standing around in the freezing cold church parking lot. I can smell her frangipani perfume over the smell of all those pine trees.

First thing she says is, "How's your Mum doing?" so I tell her, "All right." Then I tell her that Dad's back and I can't help smiling. That's when she says she knows and her eyes get all misty and dreamy, so I change the subject, ask her where she's headed to all dressed up.

"To hear the Messiah," is what she says. Wayne and Dad are back before I can ask her what she means.

"Hello Wayne," she says, looking at him.

Wayne says, "Hi, Miss Penny."

Then Miss Penny's voice gets all soft and she says, "Merry Christmas, Fred," and Dad just grins. Santa (Father Paul in that suit) comes ho-ho-ho-ing from between two trees, dragging a long skinny Christmas tree wrapped in a green mesh net.

Wayne pulls a face, says, "The thing's frozen solid, Diane."

"But it's a cultivated tree," Dad tells us all. "A top-of-the-line tree, right Wayne? Father Paul?"

Father Paul says, "Ho-ho-ho-right, Fred." Wayne doesn't say anything; he shakes his head instead.

Wayne and I get into the car with the tree, and Wayne says to me in a quiet voice that the tree could be as bald as Granny without her wig on for all we know and winks. Granny doesn't know that Wayne and I saw her without her wig on, one day from the backyard when she took the thing off to vacuum it. I nod my head and wish we'd had the chance to look the tree over for bald patches before buying it.

Dad gets in the car too and says, "What a great tree, eh Wayne?"

Wayne folds his arms across his chest, says, "That tree doesn't even smell like a tree."

"It'll thaw!" Dad says enthusiastically and starts up the engine. He backs up the car, makes a big deal out of almost running down Miss Penny and her tree. He gets out of the car and Wayne says, "Look how puny her tree is, Diane," so I turn around and look.

There's Dad, grinning again and taking the tree out of Miss Penny's arms and carrying it to her car. It fits in her back seat like a glove. Dad comes back over to us and when he opens the car door, we hear Miss Penny's voice saying, "See you at the party then, Fred."

We both look at Dad and he shrugs his shoulders, says, "I invited her to the big party on Christmas Eve."

Wayne says, "Why did you do that, Dad?"

And Dad says, "It's Christmastime, Wayne. Jesus Christ, ease up a little will you?"

We get to stay up a while at the party, at least until everyone arrives. Dad's manning the bar, fixing cherry Cokes for Wayne and me, putting extra cherries at the bottom, and Virgin Marys for Mum. The Lesters are the first to arrive and when Dad takes Mrs. Lester's fur, he holds a piece a mistletoe over her head and says, "Truce?" Mrs. Lester scowls and kisses him lightly on the cheek, then goes off to help Mum in the kitchen with the party food.

Mr. Lester goes, "Women, eh Fred? She'll come 'round." Dad nods at him and puts the mistletoe back in his pocket for later. He and Mr. Lester move over to the bar and start fixing drinks for each other.

Granny and Miss Penny arrive together, though Wayne says he's pretty sure they didn't come together.

"How do you know?" I ask him. Wayne says he overheard Granny ask Dad, "What in hell is she doing here?" and, "Who the hell invited her?" Granny usually never says hell once in a conversation, never mind twice.

Wayne says, "I've got to keep my eye on Dad, Diane," like it's some kind of special mission he's on and goes off to help Dad and Mr. Lester fix drinks. I don't know why Wayne thinks he has to watch Dad, but I say, "You do that, Wayne," wishing he'd go away and stop trying to spoil things.

Miss Penny is wearing a slinky black dress with diamonds up one side. She says they aren't real.

"They're rhinestones," she says to me and her voice seems to purr like a cat's.

Dad comes over and tells us to say good night to everyone because Santa will be here soon. Over the radio, the weatherman says he's seen an unidentified flying object on the radar screen that looks to be a sleigh and eight tiny reindeer. Mum says that's our cue to go to bed.

Wayne says, "Baah, he's just making that up. There's no such thing as Santa Claus and Jesus wasn't even born on Christmas day."

Mum goes, "That's enough, Wayne," looking at me.

I go into the fridge for carrots. Wayne's said that Santa doesn't exist and he's really Dad. He knows this for a fact because last year neither of them showed. All the same I leave a plate of carrots for the reindeer and cookies and milk for Santa. Dad comes in the kitchen with a glass in his hand and says, "See you in the morning, Wayne," but his voice sounds weird.

On our way upstairs, Wayne says maybe he's been wrong about Dad all along and maybe this time will be different. Wayne sits on the end of my bed until I fall asleep to the sound of far away laughter.

We Could Stay Here All Night

In the morning, no one mentions Dad, but he clearly isn't around. There's an empty Five Star whiskey bottle on the table next to the uneaten carrots. A cigarette butt with pink lipstick on one end of it floats in the glass of milk. Wayne gets to the whiskey bottle first, peels off the star and sticks it to his pyjamas. Mum comes in the kitchen, smoking a cigarette. Her eyes are bloodshot and puffy. She looks at the two of us sitting there, at the plate of carrots on the table.

We don't get the things we want. Mum says Santa must have got our house mixed up with another house on the street. But I feel like whoever left these gifts here didn't even know us.

Wayne doesn't get a hockey stick. He gets a Stargazer's Weather Set and a tabletop telescope instead. I get a globe with a light bulb inside so it doesn't even spin and a pink travel case with my initials on the handle. Mum gets a portable vacuum cleaner and a card with a lot of fifties in it that fall out when she opens the card. Wayne says, "At least now we can vacuum them up, eh Mum?" The fifties, or the vacuum, or something Wayne says, makes her cry.

Granny comes over while we're all still in our pyjamas opening presents and there's a lot of whispering going on all of a sudden. She brings itchy sweaters and brand-new five dollar bills for Wayne and me.

Mum says, "We're skipping Mass today on account of the sleet," so I put my Christmas dress away and Wayne throws his good shoes into the back of the closet for next year.

Wayne and I watch from the living room window until Granny tells us to get away from there and not to mention

Dad during dinner. Mum stays in her bathrobe all day and spends most of the time in her bedroom with the dog. Wayne and I tiptoe by the closed door a couple of times, but we don't hear anything on the other side except for a few sniffles. I say that maybe Dad's in there with her and they're not feeling too well, but Wayne says Dad's gone again and maybe for good this time.

By afternoon the sleet changes to rain and the rain forms a hard shiny surface on the snow already on the ground. Wayne and I take his telescope out into the yard. Our boots break through the crusty snow with a *thuck, thuck* sound. But there aren't any stars to gaze at so we spend our time punching our boots in the snow, until we have punched down all the snow in our yard, trying to break through.

The Comfort Zone

All my life we'd lived in St. Lambert, a canal lock on the St. Lawrence Seaway—a shortcut from the Great Lakes to the Atlantic—and nothing ever happened there. Then one night in October of 1970, the police cordoned off a ten block radius right in our neighbourhood, and Dad said he had a feeling something was about to happen. We got caught up in it on our way back from my grandmother's with Dad at the wheel, even though he had another six month suspension, and no valid driver's licence.

"Everybody sit tight," Dad said as a QPP officer approached our car. Dad's eyes were red from too little sleep, and his voice was still hoarse from the argument he'd started with Granny. My brother and I watched from the back seat.

"Fred, don't," Mum said, but he was already standing in the street. The policeman seemed edgy. He'd wanted my father to stay put too. But they talked for a few moments, with the officer doing most of the talking in broken English while Dad listened, then the two of them walked around to the back of our car. Dad opened the trunk. Through the back window, Wayne and I spied on them, but could only see their belts. Dad's belt, a gift from Granny, and too long by six inches, wagged at us like a tongue.

But for once they weren't after Dad, they were looking for a man named Pierre Laporte, who was the Labour Minister in the Quebec government, and missing.

"Why him?" Mum said, as Dad got back in the driver's seat, and tucked his belly under the steering wheel.

"Beats me," Dad said, almost disappointed.

We didn't find out the real story until we got home and were sitting in the living room in front of the TV with our roast beef dinners on our laps. The poor man had been kidnapped—snatched right off the street in front of his house and folded into a car—with the neighbours and his wife and everybody watching.

"Imagine, just standing there," Dad said. He wiped gravy off his chin with the back of his hand. "Why didn't somebody do something?"

Just then the phone rang and we all jumped.

Mum said, "Don't anybody move. I'll get it." She put her plate on the coffee table and went into the kitchen. We heard her answer and then her voice grew quiet. She slid the door between the kitchen and the hallway shut.

"That'd be your granny, I bet," Dad said with a "tsk."

After that, driving was tricky. We had to drive three blocks out of our way to church, five blocks out of our way to school. The cemetery was completely off limits so we didn't go there at all anymore, and Granny's second husband—a man we visited called old Bill—would have to wait.

Granny said tough times called for drastic measures, or some kind of measures, but not too many people in our neighbourhood agreed with her.

Mum began driving us to and from school after that. She split the driving with Mrs. Templeton from across the street. Mrs. Templeton was a better driver than Mum, who drove almost three miles out of her way to avoid the roadblocks some days and never took the same route twice. But Mrs. Templeton pointed her car in the same direction every morning and headed straight for the Laporte's house on Robitaille Street.

Because of Mrs. Templeton we all got our first good look at soldiers with helmets, semi-automatic rifles, and tanks.

"Yoo hoo," Mrs. Templeton said. She cracked open her window and waved. One of the soldiers approached our car. "Any news?" she said.

"*Pas encore*," the soldier said. Patty, who was bilingual like her mother, translated for Wayne and Frankie and me.

"Nothing," Patty said. "They haven't heard anything."

"Bummer," Wayne said. He and Frankie Lester sat in the back seat of the Coupe together talking about camouflage outfits and guns, while Patty and I squeezed up front next to her mother who was wearing too much makeup for that time of day.

Mrs. Templeton smiled and craned her neck to see what

was going on, on the other side of the barricade. But we weren't allowed to get very close. From our vantage point, we saw mostly troops standing around drinking coffee, eyeing Mrs. Templeton.

"*C'est dommage*," she whispered to the soldier.

"Tough luck," Patty whispered to me.

Mrs. Templeton backed the car down the street and said, "*À demain*," in her best voice. Patty said we'd be coming back the next day.

Granny came to live with us around the same time that poor man was kidnapped because she said her TV was on the blink again. Mum said Granny had cabin fever, that's all, from being cooped up in her apartment all day. Granny's apartment on Logan Street fell within the boundaries of the roadblock, so getting in and out was a big deal.

"Imagine searching an old crone's purse," Granny said to me. She snapped open her purse and I peeked in. "Angina pills and Kleenex," she pointed out. Then she pulled out a wrinkled dollar bill from the secret compartment and handed it to me. "Don't tell your brother," she said.

Dad started in with the beer and tomato juice the morning he helped Granny move her things into Mum's sewing room, but he told us that she wasn't staying. "Just until this thing blows over, Ruth," he said to Mum. "Not one day more." Granny had a hard time seeing what Mum called Dad's "potential."

At our house, Granny always said she was too cold, and

would make for the thermostat at the end of the hallway. Dad would pass her in the hallway on her way back.

"We can't afford to heat the whole goddamned neighbourhood!" he'd shout. "I'm a boiler maker, not a millionaire!" Then he'd crank it to where we liked it—a red dash on the thermostat called The Comfort Zone. This went on most nights, when Dad wasn't out in the backyard spotting Huey helicopters through binoculars or sleeping it off on the sofabed in the cold room.

People started staying up all night. The police tapped the telephone lines, so we couldn't use the phone anymore. After a bomb scare, Mum told us to make wide arcs around mailboxes or better still to cross the street entirely. And I watched her open our letters gingerly, with the tip of her finger. Then one morning our copy of the *Montreal Gazette* reported that we weren't allowed to gather in crowds of more than four.

"We're a crowd?" Mum said. She was sitting at the kitchen table, winding her hair up in curlers and looking at the newspaper. Wayne and I were sitting at the table beside her, and Dad and Granny were near the fridge arguing and elbowing each other like mad. She pulled her two hands out of her hair and put her face in them. The whole kitchen smelled like Dippity-Do.

Dad went over and took her in his arms. He said, "There, there, Ruth," but Mum wanted to pack up and move to Toronto.

"I can't live like this," she said.

"It's okay, so what if we're a crowd?" Dad said. But suddenly, we couldn't go out together anymore either. If Dad went to the beer store, he took just me. Wayne went with Mum while Granny stayed at home, minding the fort.

That Monday afternoon Dad got a call from his local. His boss said there was a job, out of town. He wanted Dad to come downtown to discuss terms.

Mum said, "Do you have to?" It was the first time since the kidnapping that any of us would venture over the St. Lawrence River and into the city. The International Brotherhood of Boiler Makers was sandwiched between a pool hall and a Classy Formal Wear shop on St. Denis Street in the east end of Montreal.

Dad said, "Money's money." He pulled on his jacket, but didn't do it up. Then he slicked one hand through his hair and brushed it behind his ear. "I won't be too long."

"What about Diane?" Mum asked, pointing at me. I was sitting on the sofa with an after-school snack on a napkin. "Why don't you take her with you?"

"Diane?" Dad said. I looked up. "Want to go for a ride and look at those suits?" I raced to the hall closet for my coat. The formal shop next door to the I.B.B.M. changed their window displays every month.

Dad took back roads and side streets all the way to the foot of the Victoria Bridge, before darting out onto the boulevard and into traffic. On the bridge, I looked out the window at the river below, at the ships moving in and out of the St. Lambert Lock, at the skyscrapers downtown. I pointed to buildings I recognized, naming them.

"Cheese grater," I said, pointing to the tall hotel Wayne and I thought looked like a giant cheese grater. Dad squinted, then smiled.

"*Le Château Champlain*," he said with a bad accent.

"Wedding cake." The wedding cake was a four-tiered building where Granny used to work as a legal secretary.

"Sunlife building."

I looked for the cross on the mountain, but before I could spot it, Dad pointed in the rear view mirror.

"Don't look now," he said. I turned around and looked out the back window. A train was rolling toward us down the centre of the bridge, and the car began to sway slightly from side to side with the motion of it. I tightened my grip on the dash. Dad kept both hands on the wheel to steady the car, and my nerves, and stared straight ahead.

When we got there, Dad asked me if I wanted to come in. The I.B.B.M. was in a smokey little hall with a bar at one end, an office at the other; it doubled as a Legion when the brotherhood wasn't using it. "Or you can stay in the car," he said, gesturing towards the tuxedo shop with his thumb. He'd parked across the street from the pool hall, but from where I was sitting I had a clear view of the bride and groom in the shop window. "You won't be scared, will you?" he asked.

I shook my head. "I'll wait here," I said.

He was gone almost an hour, and it was pitch dark out when he spilled back onto the street. For company, I'd listened to the radio the whole time, turning the dial every few minutes, looking for English stations and songs I recognized, until it conked out.

When he couldn't get the engine to turn over, Dad went into the hall again, but came back out almost right away with another man. "This man's going to give us a jump start, Diane," he said. His breath was sour. "That's all we need." The other man waved hello, and then got into the car behind us. He plugged his car into ours, Dad turned over the engine, and we were off again—swerving all over the road.

On the way back, the bridge was up to let an ocean freighter through, so we had to swing around the other way. "Good goddamn," Dad said, pulling onto the autoroute, but he kept his speed down, and we cruised home at an even fifty, and counted ourselves lucky.

When the police figured out that the kidnappers had switched cars a couple of times, everyone was a suspect. They showed up on our block, peering in car windows and knocking on doors. Dad and I were out back listening to the *chop, chop, chop* of the Voyageurs when they came looking for our car. According to the English CBC, the police were looking for a dark green Chevy.

Dad said we had an Impala. "And as you can see," he said, pointing to our car, which had been left half on the curb, half on the street, "It isn't green."

The police didn't care what colour our car was. They asked him to unlock the door, so that they could have a look inside.

"It's open," Dad said, his eyes still skyward. "See for your-self." On the front seat of the car, they found a Molson's can that was still cold. They held the can up under Dad's nose. "*Qu'est-ce que c'est?*" one of the policemen asked, and even I knew what that meant.

"Beer can," Dad said. "*Bière froide.* Beer." He gestured with one of his hands and his head tipped back, then winked at me. "*Glug, glug, glug,* you know." *Bière froide, chien-chaud, patates frites*—all phrases he'd memorized off *dépanneur* windows as he sped by on his way home. He taught them to me: cold beer, hot dogs and French fries—words to remember in case I got lost in the Frenchy part of town. Then, reassured I would never starve, he told me he could sleep nights. (It was Mum who taught me my telephone number, and late at night I practised in the dark—*six-sept-deux-neuf-neuf-trois-six*—until the numbers rolled off my tongue and I sounded like a native.)

The policemen smiled at each other before tossing the beer can to Dad who caught it with his free hand. Then they looked in the trunk of the car again, but didn't turn up anything else that interested them. I turned up a Barbie who had been missing since summer. She'd lost a pink shoe.

Wayne came back from the hockey arena lugging sticks and skates as the policemen were heading over towards the Lesters.

"Awww," Wayne said, afraid he'd missed something big.

For that week only, Dad and Wayne and I had to let Granny have her way with the TV so we ended up watching "Hymn

Sing" with her on Sunday night, which was a religious variety show with a lot of singing and not too much variety. Granny's other favourite show was "Coronation Street" which she usually watched in the afternoons when Wayne and I were in school, and thank God. We all watched the ten o'clock news together though, and Mum let me stay up as late as Wayne.

The announcer read the first note from the kidnappers on TV. It was the one they found at the Peel Street *métro* station and they called it a *communiqué* which Dad said was a French word for note. Then they wised up and started keeping things secret. This set Dad off again. We glued ourselves to the French TV station to try and find out what was going on, but no one's French was very good.

"Eh?" Granny said, "What did he say?"

Mum went, "Sshhh, I can't hear, Mum."

Dad cranked up the sound on the TV so loud that the reporter was practically screaming the news at us, but we still couldn't understand a word he said. We finally switched over to the English station when the hockey news came on because my brother Wayne didn't want to miss a word of that, then Mum said, "Time for bed."

As usual, Mum just tried to make the best of a bad situation, smoking a lot of cigarettes and dropping them into Dad's half empty beer cans when he wasn't looking. She poured tumblers of Dubonnets for Granny, which was a fancy French drink Granny took over cracked ice. She moved her sewing machine into their bedroom and spent a lot of time in there working on our Halloween costumes.

I was going to be a Chinese toadstool, which was an idea

Mum got from a ladies' magazine, but she hadn't let me see my costume yet. It was blue though, satin with sparkles sewn around the hem, she'd promised. Wayne was a bum, and Mum shortened an old pair of Dad's blue jeans and ripped holes in the knees for him. Frankie Lester was going to be a bum, too—all the boys were bums—and my friend Patty was going to be a housewife this year. I was a housewife last year.

Because of the curfew, we were all trapped in the house like shut-ins. Nobody was allowed to go out after dark, and the police drove up and down the streets with their lights on, but not their sirens. Our street was safer than most though, with the provincial Department of Roads across the street and the Royal Canadian Mounted Police parked out front in their unmarked car. Wayne said they were sitting ducks in that grey sedan. "Standard issue," he said, which was something he'd heard Linc say to the captain on the "Mod Squad" the night before. Linc Hayes was Wayne's favourite, and Julie Barnes was mine.

He'd come up with this theory about the significance of the letter X on their licence plate, too, and we ran around the neighbourhood as Linc and Julie and looked for other unmarked cars when we weren't stuck inside. We found two on Green Avenue and spotted another on *L'espérance*. Dad said they might as well have painted the words "Undercover Cops" right on the roof of their car, or better still, stamp it on their foreheads. But Mum and Granny and I liked having them there, and Mum said over dinner she thought she'd miss them when they were gone.

"Hear that, Jean Guy?" Dad shouted in the direction of

the street. Dad called lots of French men "Jean Guy," though Mum said it wasn't entirely flattering.

The sewing room was right next door to my room, and I could hear Granny stumbling up the hallway to the bathroom and back most nights. The first night she even came in to my room and switched on the light, with her nightie already hiked up around her hips and her knees bent. But it was by accident. She said, "It's just Granny, Diane," even though I could see exactly who it was plain as day, and then, "Go back to sleep." But I couldn't sleep, couldn't stop thinking about poor Monsieur Laporte.

Then one night someone popped a bullet through Wayne's bedroom window in what the police later called "an unrelated incident." I woke up to the sound of a loud crack, then sirens screaming past our house. Dad came to get me, and Wayne was with him carrying the bullet in the palm of his hand and smiling. "Neat, eh?" he said, sharing the little bullet with me.

We tiptoed past the sewing room and Granny, who had somehow managed to sleep through the racket, and crept downstairs to Mum. We didn't turn on any lights because we didn't want to attract any more attention to our house, and instead huddled together in the downstairs hallway with a flashlight. Dad brought us ice cream sandwiches from the freezer in the cold room and we all sat there in the dark eating. Then he told a knock-knock joke that cracked Mum up and he had to kiss her to keep her quiet.

"Let's not wake up Granny," Wayne said, which was what we were all thinking anyway. Mum nodded her head, too, with tears welling up in her eyes and ice cream melting down her forearm and Dad's lips resting there on her lips. Then it was all over, and the neighbourhood was still again, and we tiptoed back to bed.

In the morning we found out that troops had been on the move the night before, taking up positions not only in our neighbourhood now, but all over the island of Montreal. Dad called the police. "Enough is enough, Ruth," he said to Mum, but his voice hesitated. Two policemen showed up and took measurements. They measured the size of the hole in the pane of glass and the size of the window, but they didn't measure the distance between Wayne's bed and the window, which wasn't very great.

They asked a lot of questions. They wanted to know if Dad was anybody special.

"I'm nobody," Dad said. His voice was still shaky, like before. "But he's my son," he said next, pointing at Wayne. Wayne was sitting next to Granny, who was sitting next to Mum. They were all on the sofa except for me. I was standing next to Dad. And Dad's hand was sometimes on my shoulder, sometimes not.

One of the policemen, the sympathetic one, said, "It will all be over soon, Monsieur."

"How the hell do you know?" Dad said.

"It's just a rumour," the policeman said. He pocketed

Wayne's bullet and straightened up.

"What is?" Dad wanted to know. The policemen glanced at each other, but they didn't say anything. We had heard the rumours though. One night the CBC reported that the poor man had already been murdered. Then they changed their minds an hour later.

"*Rien*," the other policeman said, which I knew meant squat.

Whatever it was, I bet it was a crazy kind of rumour. But there were lots of crazy rumours around. Like cancelling Halloween. I thought cancelling Halloween was almost like cancelling Christmas.

Dad said, "Jesus Christ." Then he went into the kitchen to fix himself a beer and tomato juice. I showed the policemen to the door. They took the bullet with them, even though Wayne wanted to keep it for a souvenir.

After they were gone, Dad was off to the barricade on foot to find out if anything was going on, and Mum was back at work on the costumes for Halloween. He came back without news and said, "Those Jean Guys are hiding something," and went outside to sulk in the backyard.

All this happened before breakfast, before Mrs. Templeton showed up, dressed to kill, to take us to school.

Wayne and I didn't tell Mum about Mrs. Templeton and the soldiers because that would have been the end of Mrs. Templeton and the carpool in no time flat.

At school, everyone was talking about sending the kidnappers to Cuba, so Miss Epp pulled down the map of North America and pointed to a small island off the coast of Florida. At this point, we were all still thinking that the bad guys would get to go to Cuba and the good guys would get to go home. Even Miss Epp thought so.

"Cuba," she said, using the pointer. Then she told us how she'd gone there with the man she almost married last year. "The beaches were nice," she said, "But the women didn't wear any tops."

When Patty heard that, she leaned across her desk and whispered to me. "Who'd marry her?" she said, which made us both giggle. Then Miss Epp glared at us, so we clammed up.

Instead of having catechism class as usual, my class marched across town to wait for Father Paul to show up and let us into church. We had been practising for our First Confession since the beginning of the school year, practising saying, "Bless me Father for I have sinned," until we had it memorized to death, because, when the time came, Miss Epp had made it pretty clear she wanted no slip-ups.

Patty and I thought Holy Confession with Miss Epp was a far cry from last year's Holy Communion with Miss Cole when even the girls got to be priests sometimes and we all got to feed each other tasty pieces of paper we called wafers. But this year, Miss Epp said, like it or not, there was only one priest and that priest was Father Paul.

That morning was the first time we were practising in real confessionals and the first time we were using a real priest. The week before, we were supposed to tell our sins to Miss

Epp in the utility closet, but when my turn came I panicked about what to say and wound up making up sins to tell her. For lying to Miss Epp, I was supposed to go straight to hell, according to Wayne.

Because we were a pretty big group, Brother Maurice showed up to help out even though he was still just a brother and wasn't a bona fide priest yet. Miss Epp split the class in two, being careful to put me in one group and Patty Templeton in the other. My group stuck with Father Paul at the front of the church, but Patty's got saddled with Brother Maurice who may or may not have known the passwords.

Before we started practising for the real thing, Father Paul said a little prayer for that poor man, and I closed my eyes and tried to pray hard, too. Then Father Paul disappeared into one of the confessionals and a tiny red light above the door went on. We were supposed to file in one by one after him.

Miss Epp said, "Why don't you go first, Diane Wilkinson," because she hated me. I slinked into the closet and clicked the door shut. Then I yanked my tunic above my knees and kneeled down on the cushion.

Father Paul slid open a little white screen and I got a good whiff of his cologne which smelled like grass clippings. He said, "Don't be nervous, Diane," even though he wasn't supposed to know who it was. But he knew who I was all right, and he knew who Wayne was too. "This is only a dry run, remember?"

But before he could say anything else, I blurted out how I'd lied to Miss Epp in the utility closet, and I'd lied to Mum about the roadblocks and Mrs. Templeton, and then finally how I'd prayed they'd find that man only so Granny would go home again to her own apartment and leave us alone.

Father Paul was quiet on his side of the confessional and I suddenly remembered how I'd forgotten to say the most important part that went "Bless me Father for I have sinned."

"Father Paul?" I whispered.

"That it, Diane?" he said in a friendly voice as if that wasn't enough.

I got two Hail Marys for my trouble compared to the stiff penalty Brother Maurice doled out to Patty for confessing to trying on her mother's negligées and who knows what else. At the communion rail, Patty kneeled down on the marble beside me and mumbled eight Our Fathers one after the other. All the while, she rolled her eyeballs and grinned. But I stayed at the rail longer than anyone and when I finally stood up, my knees were flat.

After confession we got to run around in the oak room in the basement of the church where Father Paul and Brother Maurice divvied up animal crackers and apple juice between us. I steered clear of both of them though, and I steered clear of Miss Epp, too.

The next morning, two more policemen showed up at the school to arrest our French teacher. But this time, they didn't even take out their badges. Later Sister Helen would call it resisting arrest, but at the time it was just Madame Boisvert shrieking at the top of her lungs, the policemen, and us.

"*Mes enfants*," she said, raising her voice. It wasn't her "*Frère Jacques*" voice with its careful attention to consonants and rolling Rs. This French voice spat out French swear words that Mum said were dirtier than ours, but only sounded sweeter because they were all about Jesus.

The policemen cornered her at the back of our room, and pressed her bum up against our cubbyholes.

"*Mon Dieu!*" she shouted at last.

After that Sister Helen took over the job of teaching French at our school even though she didn't speak French.

Then two nights later, a French TV reporter discovered the man's body. Dad said the reporter got an anonymous tip over the telephone. "What a story," he said.

They found the man's body in the trunk of an old black car. The car had simply rolled onto the St. Hubert air force base which was not too far from where we lived.

I got what I prayed for. Granny went back to her apartment on Logan Street and for a while everything went back to normal. Dad went on the wagon again, until Granny had her second stroke and came to live with us for good, and he fell off.

They didn't cancel Halloween after all, but instead restricted it to daylight hours and Wayne and I had to go out in the middle of a Saturday afternoon when most people were out shopping for groceries at the Dominion. Wayne said he felt too old for trick or treating that year, but Mum made him go with me anyway. We ran into three other kids on our regular route, all of them dressed like soldiers.

We didn't get very many treats. Mum tried to make up for

it by stuffing our fat plastic pumpkins with leftover candy when we got back, but it wasn't the same.

"What do you say?" she asked us as she swung open the door. She held the treats in the air above our heads and pretended not to recognize us—the same thing she did every year. We were supposed to say, "Trick or treat." But that year, looking at us in broad daylight, she wasn't fooling anybody. We stayed quiet as we hustled past her into the house, anxious to get inside where it was warm, safe.

Lent

The new sponsor's name was Miss Petts and she was over that first Thursday in Lent. There was a blizzard outside, but inside where we were sitting getting to know each other, it was warm. My father had been on a bender, and there were dark stains under his eyes, but now he was sober again and full of remorse. This time, he was swearing to lay off the hard stuff for good. It was 1974 and I was twelve years old.

"So help me, God," my father said out loud, and he sounded desperate. My father did not believe in God and had never found much use for Him or His Church, so it struck me as strange that this time he was asking for His help. I crossed my fingers, then uncrossed them.

Miss Petts told us she'd been on a bender or two herself before finding A.A. I watched as she lifted one bare leg over the other and set it gently down. Miss Petts' legs were the colour of well-done steak from a vacation she'd taken on an island in the middle of the Caribbean Ocean. The island, she said, was named after a saint.

Across the room, my father's hands shook as he tilted back his seventh cup of black coffee. My mother put one hand in the direction of her Cameo cigarettes, just out of reach on the coffee table.

Outside, the wind swirled the snow into circles like small tornadoes that touched our window pane, then blew apart. I looked back at Miss Petts.

"Anyway," Miss Petts said, "I got drunk one night and I stayed drunk for a month." She took a sip of her coffee and I noticed that her hands did not shake. According to Father Paul, Miss Petts was a rock. If she couldn't help him, nobody could.

In the winter of 1974, Father Paul ran the A.A. meetings in the basement of our church, and everyone, including non-believers like my father, was welcome. That year the meetings had coincided with my brother Wayne's Cub Scout night, but my brother confided that once the meeting was called to order, all they did was sit around smoking cigarettes and telling each other sad stories. "One night they set off the smoke detector," Wayne had told me. "And everyone laughed." The rest of the time, he'd said, they took turns listening.

"Believe it or not," Miss Petts said, "I lost forty pounds." Miss Petts, who did not look to me as if she weighed all of forty pounds soaking wet, gestured down the length of her torso with one hand. My father said, "Uh uh." Then my mother went into the kitchen for the percolator and I passed around the plate of deviled eggs.

Because of Lent, we'd all given up the things we loved. My mother gave up driving the long complicated routes through our neighbourhood she'd invented to keep running errands from becoming boring. I gave up bologna sandwiches. And every Sunday before Mass, my brother reluctantly slid ten cents from his allowance into a Lenten calendar he would drop into the collection basket Easter morning. Together we were hoping to inspire my father to stay on the wagon.

Miss Petts stood up to stretch those legs. Near the piano, she admired a picture of my father pulling a rabbit out of a black top hat. She told my father she used to watch his magic show on TV. "I've never met a real magician before," she said.

My father was no magician, though it was true that he'd once hosted a television magic show for the local CBC station. Before that, he'd worked as a shore linesman for the St. Lawrence Seaway Commission until he slipped into the drink after a liquid lunch and was quickly canned. And before that, as now, he was a boiler maker.

The magic show was called "The Hocus Pocus Show," and it ran for eight episodes during the fall of 1973, in the half-hour before "Tween Set" (a pre-teen question and answer show), until my father appeared on the air with his turban on backwards and a fifth of Canadian Club up his sleeve. It was replaced by "Magic Tom," a glitzy hour-long smoke and mirrors number fronted by a man in a tuxedo and real rabbits. "Magic Tom" found the audience that had tuned out my father, and Tom went on to become the big star while my father went on the bender that had lasted until Lent.

"Fred?" Miss Petts said quietly. My father stared blankly at our new television set, which was not on. Then he cleared his throat and told Miss Petts in a crisp tone of voice that "The Hocus Pocus Show" had been axed. "Mid-season," he told her.

Miss Petts sat down on the piano bench next to my father and a plate of soft cheese. She trailed a painted fingernail along the white keys. Miss Petts was my piano teacher.

"How come?"

"The demographics were all wrong," he said, which was what he liked to tell people back then. "The ten- to fourteen-year-olds who tuned in early for "Tween Set" weren't interested in sleight of hand. They wanted facts."

"Oh?" Miss Petts said, though I remember thinking at the time that she did not believe him.

That Lent, Miss Petts told my father that there were rules. My father thought rules were for children. He said he was not a child. "I'm a leader, not a follower," he said. Nevertheless, Miss Petts said, if he was committed to staying sober he would have to attend A.A. meetings. He would have to give up boiler making for the time being to stay close to home. He would have to make an effort.

"One day at a time?" said my father.

Miss Petts told him not to worry about tomorrow. "Don't look for trouble, Fred," said Miss Petts. "It'll find you soon enough." She suggested he try a hobby. "Something to keep your mind off getting tight all the time."

Beside him, I said, "Like what?" I tried to imagine him corking or rug-hooking. He was all thumbs.

Miss Petts seemed to mull it over as she leaned down to zip up her leather boots. The fur caught. "Damn it all," she said, then she stood up. "What about piano? I could teach you."

My father told Miss Petts he liked to sing, which was true, but that he was tone deaf—a disability that had never stopped him before. For the past year, he'd sung every Thursday night while a heavy man I called Uncle Jimmy accompanied him on our piano. Between the two of them, they knew "Take Me Home Again, Kathleen," and "Goodnight Irene," and another song with a girl's name in it.

"Think about it," Miss Petts said.

"I will," my father said. Then I helped Miss Petts shrug on her beige coat as my father stood with his arms limp by his sides, watching.

"Is this camel?" I asked her. I'd prayed for a camel coat.

Miss Petts stroked the sleeve of her coat with one hand as if it were still alive. "Yes, it is," she whispered. Then Miss Petts stepped out into the cold and the snow, and picked her way down our still-icy path to her car, parked near the snowbank in front of our house. After she drove away, my father went out into the yard. Through the window I watched him pushing snow around on the end of an aluminum shovel. His face looked pale and cold, but even when the snow changed to hailstones the size of communion hosts, he did not come inside.

For twelve years, we lived in the same brick house across the street from the provincial Department of Roads where Uncle Jimmy worked. Uncle Jimmy wasn't really anybody's uncle.

He was a friend of my father who cruised the neighbour-hood in a pale blue Woody station wagon on the lookout for potholes and chipped sidewalks. (It was Uncle Jimmy who'd arranged to have our front yard filled in with concrete.)

Our house sat at the end of a dead-end street, and in a corner of our yard a sign said *cul-de-sac*. The house had five bedrooms and two staircases, a front set, and a back set that was reserved for servants.

Miss Petts believed in removing temptation. By morning, my mother had packed up all the bottles that had been in our china cabinet. She told me to drop the bag at Uncle Jimmy's on my way to school.

Outside, it was still snowing. I stuck out my tongue and caught a huge wet flake, then another and another. Standing in the middle of our dead-end street, I let my mouth fill up with snow. Then I trudged to Uncle Jimmy's house. In my arms, the bottles clinked out a song.

At his house, Uncle Jimmy told me to come in and make myself at home. Then he appeared in the doorway of his small kitchen. He was wearing a pressed white shirt and grey slacks and he smelled like a moth ball. I told him he looked nice, which he did, then I handed him the bag. "My father's turned over a new leaf."

"Another one," Uncle Jimmy said flatly. He put the bag on the counter next to a stack of bologna sandwiches. The stack was taller than I was. My mouth watered.

"Bologna," I said.

Uncle Jimmy said, "Yup." He told me to help myself. So when Uncle Jimmy went to let his cat out, I swiped the entire stack into my schoolbag.

By the time I got home from school, my father had discovered the missing bottles and the house was dead quiet. I knew they were fighting, although I wished their fights resembled the fights I'd watched on TV. I pictured my mother, impeccably dressed with perfect nails and frosted hair and skin that never blemished, throwing tantrums, then good china. But the imagined fight was loud, vocal, nothing like the real fight that seemed to take place in absolute silence.

I slipped into the hall closet with my schoolbag. The hall closet was made of cedar. The closet was full of winter clothes in the summer and summer clothes in the winter. Sitting there amongst my mother's old swimsuits and summer dresses, I pretended I was somewhere warm and tropical. Then I discovered a bottle of Southern Comfort tucked inside a rubber boot. The bottle was half-empty and I took a sip. It was sticky and sweet and rough on the throat. I tucked the bottle back inside the boot and I fished a sandwich out of my schoolbag. I took a small bite. Then I took another bite, and another, and kept on biting and listening to the silence on the other side of the door. My father found me there an hour later, wearing my mother's old choir robe, half a bologna sandwich tucked up one wide sleeve.

Later my father and I took our places at the kitchen table as if nothing had happened. He'd cleaned me up, let me swish my mouth with his Listerine. The incident was our little secret. When he was drinking, he said, he used to space his drinks and take plenty of water inbetween. He told me the trick was to learn how to drink without getting drunk, eat without over-eating.

In the kitchen my mother was at the stove, arranging frozen fish sticks on a warped pan, and my brother was already helping himself to the Jell-O salad.

"What's for dinner?" my father asked.

My mother shook her head. "Fish sticks."

"I could sure go for a nice steak," my father said cheerfully.

We did not talk during dinner. I thought that somebody should say something and that the somebody should be me. I thought about what to say. I thought about school. My head pounded and my stomach churned. I thought about religion class and how when Sister Helen had doled out Stations of the Cross for our Easter project I got the station of stations—Jesus rising triumphantly from the dead. I went over the day in my head, but I didn't say anything. My father rolled a lonely pea over toward a fish stick with the tip of a steak knife, then rolled it back. My brother coughed into his hand and looked at what he'd brought up. I felt a pit at the bottom of my stomach.

When my mother asked me why I wasn't eating, I told her about the pit. I told her the pit was making me feel sick. Across the table, my father looked up from his fish stick and winked.

I said, "Mum, I have a fever."

My mother flattened a palm against my forehead. "You're not hot," she said.

"But I'm sick," I said.

After dinner, I dipped my fingers in an ashtray and pretended it was Ash Wednesday again. I painted a sooty cross on my forehead. Then I ran through the house and I blessed everyone, even my father as he dozed on and off on the sofabed in the cold room. Afterwards, I went upstairs and lay across my unmade bed. I folded my hands over my heart and felt it beat. Then I prayed, but I did not pray for the usual things: a camel coat, a cute boyfriend, longer hair. At that moment I prayed to start Lent over. I would have given anything if only we could all start over.

On Good Friday, after a fifth of scotch, he blacked out and took the car up onto the curb and creamed a telephone pole. I was in the living room, clipping out my paper Station when my mother came into the room wearing her good car coat. She said we had to go, but she did not say where. I told her I did not want to go anywhere. I wanted to stay. I wanted to stay near the rain-streaked window, where Jesus rose triumphantly from the dead in the palm of my hand.

She told me an ambulance had picked my father up on Union Street and taken him to the psychiatric ward of the Montreal General Hospital. "They thought he was crazy this time and not just drunk," she said. She said he'd broken a leg.

We went by taxi. On the way to the hospital, we had to detour around our Impala which was parked in the middle of one of the busiest intersections in our neighbourhood. The driver slowed to look at the car. My father's hat was still in the street.

On the other side of the Jacques Cartier bridge, we passed an Easter Fair being set up in a huge vacant lot. My mother spotted the bumper cars first. She told the driver to wait for us.

When the bell sounded, my mother peeled her car off the wall. But as I tried to steer over to where she cruised in and out of traffic, I got caught in a clump of broken cars and I had to wait until the attendant hitched a ride to where I sat stalled. I watched my mother cream one little kid after another. She plowed into everyone, even the attendant as he cut a path back across the floor to his panel of controls. When the second bell sounded, the cars died just as I touched my mother's pink bumper. "Hit you," I said lamely.

Afterwards, once we were back in the taxi and again on our way to the hospital to see my father, she told me in the real world of automobiles and accidents, my hit was known as a fender bender. She was right. I'd seen my father bump cars harder in the liquor store parking lot before speeding away.

At the hospital, the doctor told us my father's liver was a lump. If my father did not stop drinking, he said, the lump would degenerate into cirrhosis of the liver. As he spoke, I stared at my father's broken leg, which was suspended in the air. The cast was still pure white because he wouldn't let me, or anyone else, sign it.

After the doctor left the room, my mother leaned over my father and began to straighten the pillows he was resting on. And although I could not see her face, I knew that she was crying.

Miss Petts turned up with a potted plant. She said tomorrow was a new day. She said they could start over. Maybe, Miss Petts suggested, my father should give prayer a shot.

"Sure thing," my father said agreeably, but all of a sudden I did not think that prayer was going to work. I could see then that my father was never going to be able to stay sober, and that my mother was going to be a bad driver the rest of her life, and that I was going to go on eating bologna sandwiches until I looked like one.

Miss Petts began the Lord's Prayer quietly to herself, then out loud. My mother looked at me, then joined in. My brother joined in, but I did not. Finally, my father joined in, and his voice was loud and full of grace. At the end of the prayer, he said, "Deliver us from evil," like he meant it.

Undertow

Claude Alouette was the third in a long line of salesmen that caught my mother's eye during those on-again, off-again years she shared with my father in Montreal. He was a shoe salesman, small potatoes when you consider what was to come later, but a good shoe salesman, kind and gentle.

Mum met Claude on the rebound, two weeks after she'd been transferred from handbags to hosiery, when her affair with the rug man fizzled out for good.

"Shag," she said. "Who needs it." She was standing up at the kitchen table, mulling over the rug swatches Henry had left behind. In her hand, she held her favourite—a deep-pile shag the colour of the Mediterranean. He'd promised wall-to-wall, eight hundred square feet of it.

"Imagine the ocean floor, Ruth," he'd said to her, stretching his hands out over our hardwoods in a big gesture.

When she told me next how she'd never loved Henry, I was glad. I thought it meant she was still carrying a torch for Dad, who by then had been gone long enough to miss my thirteenth birthday and Wayne's fifteenth.

"Me neither," I said. Henry hadn't said a pleasant word to me or my brother the entire four months he'd kept a toothbrush here. He was gruff, linty, rank with the smell of foam underlay.

Mum sent the rug swatches sailing into the garbage pail with one swipe of her arm. "Hardwood's nice, too," she said, but I don't know why she said that; she was always cursing it when she snagged her stockings, or when Wayne and I came to her with splinters in our feet.

Claude Alouette was different, though. My mother swore he wouldn't make promises he couldn't keep, like Henry had, and like my father had before him. She still thought you could trust a salesman.

"Make sure everyone knows what you sell," she told me. "That's his motto." She was sitting on the edge of her bed trying on shoes when I'd walked into the room. My mother had been hard-pressed her whole life to find a shoe that fit because she had narrow feet and high arches. When she could get it, she took a size 10 AAA and was forced to shop at Big & Tall, Tall Girl and order untested merchandise from American catalogues that specialised in larger women.

But now at her feet, in boxes from the department store where she worked, were dozens of pairs of shoes in her size: fancy beaded pumps for night time, sensible flats for day time. The flats came one in every colour.

"A colour for every day, a shoe for every occasion," she sang, easing her feet into a pair. She'd even helped herself to complimentary hose to go with the shoes—Whisper control tops, Secret all-in-ones, L'eggs. Finally, she settled on a pair of pumps and stood up. "Like 'em?" she whispered.

They were exquisite. All gold. Even the heels were gold. But instead of drooling over the shoes, I asked, "Is Claude single?" Henry, who'd been married twice, had daughters my age. Once over a holiday weekend, I'd overheard Mum fantasizing to him about reuniting us all under the same roof like the Brady Bunch—Wayne and me and Henry's four daughters padding around on deep-pile carpeting.

"Claude's divorced," she answered happily, as if divorce was this wonderful state we should all be lucky enough to find ourselves in one day.

My brother, tiptoeing down the hallway in his ice skates, said, "Isn't that a sin?" Wayne used to be an altar boy in our church and thought of himself as an expert on sin.

"Sin, schmin," Mum said, tapping another Cameo cigarette out of her pack. She told him to take his skates off. "You can't ice skate in the house, Wayne," she called after him. Then she wandered into the bathroom, watching her feet as she went, and picked up a curling iron sizzling in a small puddle of water on the vanity. In a moment, I heard her cry out, "Oh."

I went to the bathroom doorway and peered in. She pulled the iron away from her neck and showed me the burn. "Does this look like a hickey, Diane?" she asked. "I hope this doesn't look like a hickey."

I examined the red smudge closely. "What does it matter?" I said. "He's divorced, remember? He's probably had lots of hickeys."

"Diane," she said, but she wasn't angry. She was distracted

with the iron, and the fuzz ball she was making out of her hair. "Hell," she said. She looked in the mirror and scowled. "What am I going to do now?"

I walked out of the room. "Wear a hat."

When I told Wayne about the new shoes, he said he was glad Mum wasn't wasting any time looking for a replacement for that bum Henry, and Dad, and a new father for us. "But a shoe salesman?" Wayne said, looking at his feet. "What about that guy from sporting goods?" My brother Wayne, who played right wing with the Midgets, wanted new ice skates with Bobby Orr's endorsement across the blades, not new shoes.

Claude showed up with a carton of duty-free cigarettes and a sandy bucket full of fresh clams he'd driven all the way across the American border into Newport, Vermont, to dig up.

"Yummy," Mum said, slapping her hands together and making a cupping sound. Wayne and I both knew she hated seafood. What's more, she'd planned the night out with Claude, not in with us.

"Yuck," I said. I pointed into the bucket. "Dirty little sea creatures swimming around in their own poop. That's what she's always saying."

Mum glared at me, and then told Claude to excuse me.

Graciously, she ate the clams while Wayne and I had macaroni and cheese. Claude steamed the clams in a bottle of cheap white wine he'd brought with him, then showed her how to scoop out the meat by using one of the clamshells instead of a fork.

I said, "We have forks, you know."

"*Nous avons des forchettes*," Mum translated.

But Claude said, "*Pas grave*," or something like that. The rest of the time, he spoke English.

During dinner, it became apparent to me that Claude Alouette had only read one single book in his lifetime and that it was his Bible. He said it was called *How to Sell Anything to Anybody* and it was written by an American used-car salesman who'd made his way into *The Guinness Book of World Records* for selling 1,425 used cars in 1973.

"Number one rule," Claude said to Wayne, "sell the sizzle, not the steak." I watched Mum's eyes perk up at the mention of steak, but then she quickly looked down at the clam in her hand. She slurped it out of the shell the way Claude had taught her, then tried to smile as the clam slipped onto her tongue.

"What does that mean?" Wayne wanted to know.

"Let me put it this way," Claude began. "Most of my customers already own a pair of shoes—a new pair is no biggy."

"So?"

"Touching them, trying them on, makes some people drool. I don't want to sell to some people. I want to sell to all people. And what makes all people drool, Wayne?"

"I don't know," Wayne said.

"Smelling it."

Mum smacked two clam shells together and they made a

hollow sound. "Oops," she said, but Wayne and Claude didn't notice; they were too busy hitting it off. I pushed the Kraft Dinner around on my plate, then lined up the noodles to spell *I'm not hungry*. I showed the letters to Mum.

"That's fine, Diane," she said, frowning.

I looked at her then, sliding one sticky clam down her throat after another, and tried to see what she saw in Claude Alouette.

"Everybody likes the smell of new shoes," Claude finally said. "Get 'em past the sticking point—let 'em smell 'em— then lock 'em up."

"All right!" Wayne said. Wayne was easily sold, but I wasn't.

Despite his obvious command of the English language, Claude Alouette still had a thick French accent. He called Mum "Root" instead of her real name, Ruth. Mum thought it was a scream.

"Isn't Claude a riot, Diane?" she'd say to me.

"A real laugh and a half," I'd say back, but Claude couldn't seem to get his tongue around Diane either, so he called me "Dee-Ann" like it was two names instead of one. My brother Wayne still got to be "Wayne" though.

After that first night with the clams, Claude Alouette became a fixture around the house, like the sofa the furniture man conned Mum into or the new hi-fi the stereo man clipped her on. After work, Claude would ride home from the department store with her and stay late. He'd rub the tired soles of her feet, teach her the French words for metatarsals and tendons and digitals, while she lounged in front of the black and white, loving every minute of it.

Claude cooked our dinner sometimes, exotic French food he'd spend hours in the kitchen preparing. One afternoon he even mixed all the Jell-O packets he'd found in the cupboards together in an attempt to discover a new flavour. It tasted like strawberry and it was the colour of mud, but Mum made us each choke down a bowl anyway, even though it stained our teeth.

Still, he wasn't very paternal. He didn't ask us about our grades, or our friends at school; he didn't remember our birthdays. He didn't even come to church with us on Sundays, but we still went. One Sunday before Collection, Mum whispered to us that Claude was a lapsed Catholic, but Claude called himself a C & E Catholic, which meant he showed up at Mass twice a year, on Christmas and Easter, all holy and repentant.

But Claude knew people. He took Mum to The Stork Club, the El Morocco, and the Mount Royal Race Track where she rubbed elbows with the mayor of Montreal. Claude brought Wayne to meet one of the Mahovlichs—Frank or Peter, I don't remember which one—in the Montreal Canadiens' dressing room after a hockey game, and Wayne got a pat on the back and an autographed puck.

Claude also made my brother a bird dog—which was a big honour in that used-car salesman's book—and paid him three dollars for every customer Wayne sent in Claude's direction.

"What if they're only looking?" Wayne asked him one evening. The two of them were sitting on the sofa, waiting on Mum, who was finishing a new hairdo in the bathroom, a soft wave with summer highlights around her face. She'd offered to do me too, but I'd declined. I liked my hair the way it was—mousy-brown and straight as a stick.

"That's okay," Claude said. "I'm not going to hose you just because somebody's only looking."

"You got a deal then," my brother said.

They shook on it, a fancy handshake with a tight grip that Claude had taught him, then Claude said, "Remember, Wayne, wherever there are people, there are customers."

"Work smart, not hard," said Wayne. He smacked his hand on the armrest and sent up a little puff of dust.

When Mum came into the room, Wayne told her Claude had just made him a bird dog. Mum smiled, then looked over at me. I was sitting on the floor with my back to them, plugged into the hi-fi with the headphones. I was listening to a Nathalie Simard record that Claude had bought to help me with my French, which he said was *incroyable*—incredible— all things considered. Mum tapped me on the top of the head. "Do you want to be Claude's bird dog too, Diane?" she shouted.

"No," I said.

She pursed her lips at me.

"Hair's sorta nice," I mumbled.

Then she yelled, "Claude has a big surprise for us!" She made me take off the headphones and join them all on the other side of the room.

"We're going to Atlantic City," Claude told us. Then he pulled Mum closer to him on the sectional and she giggled.

On the morning of the big trip, Claude announced that he and Mum would sit in the front seat together and take turns behind the wheel. *"Bonjour, Dee-Ann, comment ça va?"* he said to me, but I didn't say anything to him. I sulked in the back seat of his pale blue Eldorado, with my arms folded tightly across my chest, and stared out the window. It was two hours to Atlantic City by plane, but Claude was afraid to fly. Driving would take more than eleven hours.

On her turn, Mum was all over the road, but mostly she straddled the slow lane and the shoulder and swerved out of the way of dead skunks and racoons. Next to me, in the back, Wayne was on the lookout for roadkill. "There's another one coming up on your right, Mum," he'd say, and she would jerk the wheel and we'd all go flying. One time she even pulled off the road entirely and we sat there idling, half on the shoulder, half in the ditch, before starting up again.

"Root?" Claude said. He was sitting on the bench seat beside her, lighting menthol cigarettes one after another and squeezing them into the space she'd make between two clenched fingers.

"I don't know what's the matter with me," she said, but I did. She was thinking about a trip we'd taken with my father, the family holiday we spent holed up together in a motel in Ocean City, New Jersey, because of hurricane Camille.

Between gusts of wind, Dad held Mum close and distracted my brother and me with two-headed coins and disappearing card tricks.

On his turn, Claude hogged the passing lane and honked the horn at anything that moved. I clammed up, despite Claude's best efforts to get me to talk to him. I had my nose buried in a book, a romance novel with a picture of a man standing in the shadow of the Eiffel Tower on the cover.

In Atlantic City I spent the first two days parked under a beach umbrella, reeking of coconut. I had a spray bottle filled with water that I misted myself with when I got hot, while on the other side of the blanket Mum and Claude spread out, trying to catch a bit of the spray.

Sometimes we went in the water. Or rather, Mum and Claude went in the water and I traipsed in after them. Wayne splashed us while Mum hung on to Claude's arm and inched her way in with a strip of zinc oxide down her nose and her new beach shoes on. She imagined every piece of seaweed was a jellyfish, and Claude had to reassure her until she'd waded through all the ocean junk that collected at the water's edge and was floating on her back with her hands clasped behind her head. Before I was born, she used to be the Quebec Junior Provincial Synchronised Swimming Champion, but that week in the ocean she didn't look like any champ to me.

Claude floated next to her, whispering words in French I didn't understand, while I circled like a shark.

Then one night, Mum went to the casinos with Claude,

leaving my brother and me to roam around in a strange country with no one in charge.

"You're leaving us alone?" I said to her, but "Oh, for heaven's sake, Diane," was all she said to me.

Wayne didn't seem to mind, though. "Have a good time, Claude," he said, following them to the door.

Later Wayne and I walked to the arcade on the boardwalk to play skee ball, but I couldn't concentrate. I looked for Mum in the crowd outside the casino, and once, briefly, I thought I saw her—leaning against a railing with her lips pressed together in a kiss and her arms outstretched in front of her. After that, most of my balls ended up in the gutter, if they didn't jump out of my lane altogether and into my brother's. One time, a ball bounced out of my lane, ricocheted off the side wall and into Wayne's two-hundred-point hole. Bells rang, lights flashed, and five tickets came screaming out of the slot like a tongue. In three hours, I collected just twelve tickets. "Bum luck," Wayne said to me.

At the redemption centre on the way back, Wayne traded in his tickets for a glow-in-the-dark yo-yo that he was too old for and a seashell billfold he planned on giving to Claude. It was made from dark brown shells, a hundred of them, and it was the type of thing our father would never have used in a million years.

I swung past a row of showcases and dragged a finger along the gleaming glass walls, leaving a streaky print. The cases were filled with souvenir coffee mugs and pennants and seashell men. "What about this?" Wayne said, pointing out a family of oddly-shaped corn-husk dolls. I shook my head and kept on moving down the row.

The man behind the counter gestured to the stuffed animals pinned to the wall behind him and called me "little lady" a few times, but I didn't see what I was looking for.

The next morning, Mum came back with strappy new sandals on her feet. She showed the sandals to Wayne and me, marching back and forth across the hotel carpet.

"Exactly my size, Diane. What do you think about that, eh?" She told me how Claude had hit the jackpot. She called him a high roller, though she did not mention what game Claude had been playing or exactly what he had won.

Mum took Wayne and me to The Sirloin Pit for breakfast that morning, while Claude stayed behind in the hotel room, taking care of some shoe business over the telephone.

On the way in, I said, "Steak for breakfast?"

"Why not? We're celebrating." Mum looped her arm through mine. "I've got a good feeling about all this, Diane," she said. "It's a whole new beginning for us." She pushed me into the revolving doors and got in the same section as me. "Wheeee," she said, swinging us around twice.

We were still eating our steaks when Claude arrived with summer shoes for all of us. I got leather ones with buckles on them just like Mum's, and Wayne got a pair to match Claude's.

"What do you two say to Claude?" Mum asked us. Wayne said, "*Merci*," and put the shoes right on the table next to his elbow. Mum went from looking at me to looking at Claude, but I chased a piece of filet around my plate with a fork, and didn't say anything.

After breakfast we went to the beach. It was about one hundred degrees out, and Mum lounged next to Claude under a beach umbrella he'd planted in the wet sand near the water's edge, and dipped her bare toes in. A few feet away from them, I watched my brother dive under the waves. Mum tossed the suntan lotion to me.

"Could it be any hotter?" she asked. "I think I'm starting to burn."

But before I could say anything, Claude piped up, offering to rub the lotion into her back and shoulders.

"All right," she said and smiled at me. I stayed where I was as Claude gingerly slipped my mother's suit straps off her shoulders and with the tips of his fingers began to make small impressions on her pink skin. He spread the lotion around expertly, crossed over her tan line and back, over and back, coaxing it into her skin. I watched him for a few minutes, then I waded into the ocean and let the current pull me under.

We Could Stay Here
All Night

Johnny goes into the *dépanneur* in Preville and I wait in the car. I tell him to hurry up, for pete's sake, because I haven't got all night, but he's gone almost twenty minutes.

It was my idea, driving all the way out to Preville for the beer, so Johnny wants three dollars from me when we get back, for my share of the gas. If it was up to him, he would have bought the beer right there in town with God-knows-who watching, but I said no because I didn't want anyone to see us together skulking around in Johnny's father's car which still reeked of the hash the old man smoked the day he was arrested for breaking and entering.

The *dépanneur* is two suburbs over from ours in a fancy French neighbourhood with sculptured hedges in front of the houses and no sidewalks. But it doesn't really matter about the sidewalks because nobody walks anywhere in Preville anyway. They all drive cars shaped like bullets.

Johnny and I go to the same high school that the English Catholic kids from Preville get bussed to. Or I should say, used to go to the same school. A few weeks ago Johnny was kicked out of our school for wearing unlaced steel-toed construction boots and rude T-shirts, even though he knew better. Johnny's like that sometimes, you have to hit him over the head with things until he gets them. So now he's at an alternative school for high-school dropouts in downtown Montreal and can wear whatever he pleases, which isn't very much sometimes. Even cut-offs, and you can't even wear cut-offs to the Protestant schools.

Johnny's new teacher's name is Pam. That's it. Just Pam. He says he's not even sure what her last name is, if she even told them.

There are eleven other kids in the alternative school besides Johnny and they all have nicknames like Wreck and Tank and Hammer. Johnny's nickname is Brain because he lasted in a regular school longer than any of them, but I'm not supposed to tell anyone.

When Johnny comes out of the *dépanneur*, he's got a two-four under one arm and a bag of Frito Lay under the other. He flexes the muscles holding up the beer and the muscles, or the song I'm listening to, or something, gives me the shivers. It's a Led Zeppelin song and when Johnny slides into the car he starts drumming his fingers on the dashboard and singing. "And she's buy-eye-ing a stair-air-way to he-heh-ven." His big finale is a burp and I can tell he's pleased with himself as he backs up out of the parking lot and down the street in his old man's car before taking it out of reverse.

He says, "I hope they fry the bastard" again, meaning his father. He's been talking about his father all night, saying the same thing, even though I've told him over and over how they don't fry anybody in Canada anymore. "Life then," he says, so I tell him how I doubt his father will serve a life sentence in prison for stealing a lousy toaster oven and a few silver forks. "All the same," he says and then asks me to stop being such a Doreen. "Please," he says.

Doreen is Johnny's best friend Eddy's girlfriend. She's in grade eleven, a grade higher than the rest of us, except for Johnny of course, since there are no grades in the alternative school, only one big class of students working together toward a common goal. Anyway, Johnny likes the alternative school way better than our school and is always saying how much cooler everybody is over there. I told him it is easy to be cool when you're allowed to wear cut-offs and use public transit and swear your head off whenever you feel like it, but he didn't say anything back.

It takes us over half an hour to get back to our neighbourhood because of all the traffic in Preville. We drive back through the main part of town and Johnny makes jokes about seeing my mum on the street so I duck down in the car and open and close the glove compartment a few times. A roach clip falls out and onto the floor, but I don't bother looking around for it and instead keep slamming the little door shut. Johnny asks me to quit fooling around because I'll fuck it up for good, but I don't.

Tonight we're taking all the beer over to Eddy Doyle's house instead of drinking it in the car as usual because last night I told Johnny I was fed up with doing it in his father's stinking Chevy.

"Great," he said. "That's just great, Doreen. Thank you for telling me that."

I didn't really have a good reason for not wanting to do it in the car anymore except that it was uncomfortable and messy. Besides which, I was tired of driving around for an hour beforehand looking for a deserted street to park on.

"Anyway, stop talking while I'm thinking, Diane," he said. Johnny had to have complete silence while he was thinking or it was no good. But he couldn't stop thinking about his old man getting arrested and start thinking about what I'd said so the two things started to get all jumbled up in his mind. "That son of a bitch," he said. "Goddamn son of a bitch. Now what the hell are we supposed to do, pray tell?" "Pray tell" was an expression the Brain had picked up at the alternative school.

It was my idea to take the beer over to Eddy's house and Johnny thought it was a good one. "Who's the Brain now, eh Johnny?"

"Stop calling me that."

On the way over to Eddy Doyle's basement, Johnny says how he hopes Mr. and Mrs. Doyle are out and I say, "Yeah, Johnny," but I doubt they'll be out because it's occurred to me that they never have any place to go. I mean, besides the supermarket and the liquor store. I like Mrs. Doyle well enough but he's no prize, as Mum would say. According to her, Mr. Doyle is a "no-good alkie" and I'm not to have anything to do with him or his good-for-nothing son. Or Johnny either, for that matter, but that's a longer story. She's forever asking me if I want to end up like her. I say Mum's doing all right. She's got an okay job in a downtown department store, and we live in an okay house even if it isn't smack dab in the heart of Preville. Anyway, I tried telling her how Eddy and his father and Johnny were all all right, but she didn't pay any attention to me, as usual.

Eddy lets us in the front door and whispers to us to be quiet because his father is asleep in the living room. So we all tiptoe past the living room and are careful not to wake up Mr. Doyle, but he'll probably wake up of his own accord sooner or later and come mooching around for beers like last time. Going past the door, I catch a glimpse of Mr. Doyle passed out on the rug in front of the TV. He's wearing that crumby long underwear again even though it isn't cold out. There are stains down the front of it and holes in the crotch. Mrs. Doyle is sitting in her housecoat on the sofa nearest the door and she smiles and waves a little wave at me as we sneak past. She says, "Have fun, kids," in a small voice before going back to staring at the TV set. There are two people moving around on the screen, but the sound is down so it's hard to know what's going on.

Doreen is in the basement already sitting on one of the car seats drinking a beer out of a bottle with the label peeled off.

She says, "Hi Johnny," but only smiles at me even though she knows my name. Doreen doesn't much like the fact that she's stuck hanging around with a bunch of grade tens just because Eddy flunked a grade. But I smile back at her anyway. She's wearing a short jean skirt and a white tank top and too much coral lipstick.

Eddy drains his beer, then opens three more out of the

case we've brought with us, with his teeth. It's a neat trick, but I've seen him do it plenty of times before. Doreen rolls her eyes at him, says, "Ed-dy," like it's two words and then helps herself to another beer from our case.

I say, "Help yourself, Doreen." Doreen uses one of the bottle openers that dangle from the ceiling like mobiles.

Eddy's basement is full of old car seats, four cars' worth, and empty Molson Export cases. But it isn't what my mother would call a furnished basement. It's only one big room with walls and floors made out of cement and bare black light bulbs hanging from the ceiling. The room has an eerie purple glow which makes our teeth look too white and Doreen's tank top see-through. She wears the same beige Wonderbra I do, except hers is almost three cup sizes bigger from the looks of it. Doreen is what the boys call "chesty," and I am what the boys call "flat."

There's a noisy water heater in one corner of the room and last summer Eddy and Johnny painted it steel grey to match everything else.

Eddy and Johnny take seats across from each other on the floor and try knocking upside-down bottle caps off each other's bottles. Johnny misses and has to take a sip of his beer, and keep on taking sips, until he knocks off Eddy's bottle cap. It's a game called Caps, but Johnny's not very good at it. He has lousy hand-eye co-ordination and keeps pegging Eddy in the chest with his cap. Eddy's starting to get pissed off.

"Sorry, Ed," Johnny says.

Eddy's practised with all those empty bottles so he's pretty good at the game. He takes a sip only when he's thirsty.

After they've been playing for a few minutes, I head upstairs because there's no bathroom on this floor. I run into Mrs. Doyle at the top of the stairs. She asks me if I'm having fun yet. I say we haven't even started anything.

Mrs. Doyle leans in my direction like she wants to tell me a secret. "I used to be just like you," she says. She's sitting on one of the chairs in the kitchen drinking something out of a coffee cup that isn't coffee. She doesn't have her teeth in.

"Really?" I say, but then kick myself for sounding surprised. From all the pictures hanging on the wall in the hallway, I know Mrs. Doyle was a nice-looking woman in her day. But she's not nice-looking anymore.

By the time I finish in the bathroom and go back down the stairs, Mrs. Doyle has her head down on the table next to the coffee cup.

Doreen and I eye each other from across the room until I say, "Wanna play caps, Doreen?" She hesitates at first, mostly because she doesn't like the taste of beer as much as she pretends she does, then she clears her throat and says she's not very good.

"Neither am I," I say.

"Okay."

I knock Doreen's bottle cap off every time, but she's as crappy as Johnny is at this game. She gets drunk quickly and licks off most of her lipstick between sips. Her bottle cap hits me on the leg and on the shoulder, but after a while she starts missing me entirely and only nicks the wall behind me.

"I dunno what's the matter with me," she says. She slurs most of her words, but I manage to get the drift of them anyway.

At some point Mr. Doyle wakes up and starts in on Mrs. Doyle. Every once in a while something heavy comes slamming into the basement door at the top of the stairs and then everything gets quiet for a while before starting up again.

Eddy says, "There they go again," and flips his bottle cap at Johnny's. Johnny's cap slips off his bottle and onto the floor.

"Again!" Johnny says. "Jesus!"

Eddy says maybe we should switch partners for a while, so Johnny and Doreen start tossing caps at each other and Eddy starts tossing caps at me. He hits me in the chest mostly, but sometimes aims the bottle cap right between my legs by holding it up to his eye and squinting down there at me. My face feels as if it's getting all red because for the first time in my life somebody besides Johnny is paying attention to me. But then all of a sudden he stops paying attention to me and gets up to put on a record.

Doreen says she feels sick to her stomach and Eddy says she can't hold her beer at all. "At least not the way you can," he says, eyeing me.

We stop playing with the bottle caps and start dancing. Eddy and I help Johnny up to his feet and he manages to twirl around a few times before falling back down on the car seats. Eddy and Doreen and I keep dancing around the room with Johnny watching us through the slits of his eyes. He tosses bottle caps at us, missing us entirely, and complains about having a headache.

Doreen says, "Poor Johnny," but Johnny's not paying any attention to Doreen and doesn't seem to hear her.

"What do you think you're doing?" Johnny says to me. I tell him I'm dancing. "With Eddy? With Eddy?" he says, puffing up his chest and trying to look angry. It surprises me to see him acting like he cares after everything that's been happening lately. But before I can say something like "Everything's going to be okay, Johnny," Eddy steps in between us and suggests we all calm down. Johnny and I look at each other and it's like we don't even know each other anymore.

"Nothing's going on, John," Eddy says, looking in my direction and smiling. "We're just having a bit of fun."

Johnny says, "Fun?" Then, "Okay, Ed, go ahead," as if he's somehow giving Eddy permission. He goes back to lobbing caps across the room, staring straight ahead. Eddy moves over to where I'm dancing and puts his hands on my hips. We dance like that for a few minutes with Johnny and Doreen in the room with us the whole time.

Upstairs the banging around gets louder and Eddy says that they should be getting tired soon.

Doreen says, "Who? Who?" but we don't answer her. Then she starts shouting about how she doesn't like being ignored. She says, "Especially by you, Eddy," like she could care less if Johnny and I ignore her. She sits down on the floor next to Johnny and starts whispering into his ear. The two of them stay like that for a while, giggling and whispering into each other's ears while Eddy and I sway back and forth across the floor.

Eddy goes over to put on a slow song and before you know it we're necking like crazy and dancing around the basement. Eddy's a better kisser than Johnny is any day and way taller. At first I say, "I don't know, Eddy," because my loyalty should be to Johnny after all, but Johnny isn't even looking at me. He is too wrapped up in Doreen to notice.

We dance over to the stairs and crawl under to the mattress that Johnny and I were planning on using earlier. It's cold and dark under the stairs and smells like a toilet.

Eddy says, "I love you" into one of my ears but I know he doesn't mean it. I squeeze him anyway and let his hands move over my body. My eyes adjust to the darkness in the little room and when I look past Eddy's head I can see shafts of light coming in through the cracks in the stairs. Eddy says, "Sshhh," and puts his finger over his lips. Then we hear clumsy footsteps coming down the stairs over our heads and Mr. Doyle's voice shouting, "You lousy kids." He stomps down the stairs, but misses one and tumbles to the floor.

For a few minutes we don't hear anything except Mr. Doyle's rough breathing. But then he's on his feet again and clumping all around the room. By the time he gets over to where Doreen and Johnny are sitting on the car seats, Doreen's shouting out and shaking Johnny. We hear her voice saying, "Johnny, wake up," and then, "Oh, hi, Mr. Doyle." He tells her to get dressed and get the fuck out of his house, so Doreen takes off up the stairs like a shot and we hear the *tack tack tack* of her high-heeled shoes over our heads. Then it sounds like Mr. Doyle starts in on Johnny because Johnny shouts out something like "Jesus, what the hell are you doing?"

Mr. Doyle starts hitting Johnny on the head with the

back of his hand and moving him in the direction of the stairs. I peek out through one of the cracks and see Johnny looking right at me with a strange expression on his face, like he's not sure what to do now. He calls out, "I'll wait for you in the car," before dragging himself up the stairs after Doreen. Mr. Doyle doesn't know what Johnny's talking about or who Johnny's talking to. He starts smacking his lips and helping himself to the case of beer, then he slams the door at the top of the stairs. We don't hear anything after that.

Eddy says, "We could stay here all night, Diane," and I think how great that would be.

Eddy fumbles with the buttons on my shirt with one hand and tries to unzip my jeans with the other, but he's as unco-ordinated as Johnny is after all. He has to ask me to do it, too. So I pull my shirt off over my head and slide out of my jeans. Eddy sits up to take off his shirt and hits his head on the stairs. "Shit," he says. Then he tries to slip off his jeans, but there's no room under the stairs to move around so I have to crawl to his feet and yank from there. I jerk each pant leg separately.

He starts kissing my neck and sticking his tongue in my ears until I can't hear anything anymore. I shut my eyes and see Johnny slumped over the steering wheel of his father's lousy car waiting for me to come out, pretending nothing has changed. Then it's in and out and in and out and when I open up my eyes there's Eddy Doyle, all bulgy-eyed and sweaty on top of me, panting like a dog. He says something that sounds to me like "Ha! Ha!" before rolling off and into the wall while I lie very still and try not to make a sound. Eddy pokes me in the stomach with his finger and says, "We must be drunk or something. You're Johnny's girlfriend."

I say, "Yeah, we must be."

Still in the Dark

There was no blood my very first time. Just me and Stanley McGoldbrick lying on an old air mattress behind a car seat in Andy Hampton's basement one Saturday afternoon. I was fifteen, in the dark still about love, having put all my faith in the wisdom imparted to me by my mother who'd once motioned me aside during a bridge game, and told me what little she knew. There was blood her first time. A few spots here and there.

She took a sip of sherry, then dipped her finger in and traced it around the edge of the glass to make it sing. "Laa," she sang out, with the same seriousness as an opera singer warming up. Then she handed me the glass and asked me if I wanted a taste. "It's sweet," she said, tempting me.

"No," I said.

Her first time was with my father, she said. She confided then that it hurt, too, but it wasn't a sharp pain; she said it was more like a dull ache, a toothache maybe, or something that's been broken for a while.

"Then I got used to it," she said, frowning.

In the basement that first time, Stanley wore a rubber he got from God-knows-where and made me close my eyes while he put it on. But he didn't know how to put it on properly because the instructions on the packet were worn off, and he'd left three inches of rubber at the tip of it. The thing slipped off in the middle of doing it.

"Stanley," I whispered, my throat starting to feel all scratchy and sore from so much necking. Stanley was still spread-eagle on top of me, crushing my rib cage and wheezing with asthma.

"What?" Stanley's voice was hoarse, too.

"Pick it up."

"You pick it up."

"No you."

Afterwards, neither of us wanted to touch it. So we left it there on the floor near the car seat, where Andy Hampton's mother found it two days later. She called it a prophylactic and flushed it down the toilet after showing it to Mr. Hampton.

Mr. Hampton gave the girls a lecture in the basement that same day. He talked about Promiscuity and Provocation and used a few more words that started with the letter P, but none of us girls had a clue what he was talking about. Patty stared at Mr. Hampton like he was a math problem.

"Eh?" she said, trying to figure him out.

But Mr. Hampton didn't have any daughters, so he couldn't relate to Patty or me or any of the girls. He thanked us for our Patience, then skedaddled up the stairs like a shot.

The lecture he gave to the boys was different. He used monosyllables mostly, lots of Uhmms, Ers & Heh-Hehs, according to Stanley. All the same, he said he'd like someone to step forward and take responsibility for the prophylactic. But no boy knew what a prophylactic was, so no boy stepped forward. Not even Stanley, who had an inkling Mr. Hampton was talking to him.

Back in the fourth grade, the nuns had shown us a single movie, a twenty-minute animated cartoon about flowers and insects that we got to bring our mums to. They handed us a detailed pamphlet about pistils and stamens, a pictorial representation of cross-pollination that my mum slipped discreetly into her purse on the way out. My brother Wayne, who was now seventeen and surly, saw a movie too, two years before I had. I remembered asking him if it was about flowers.

"Flowers? No, it was about dinks and hair."

"Hair? What about hair?" I ran my hand through my own hair, pulled it together between my thumb and my forefinger. It smelled like Herbal Essence.

"And my voice. It was about my voice, too."

"What about it?"

He looked at me with the if-you-don't-know-I'm-not-going-to-tell-you look that he'd given me my whole life. "Don't ask me, ask Mum."

"Mum told you?" I asked, wondering why she was telling Wayne things and not telling me.

"Dad did before he left," he said. "Dad tells me, Mum tells you. That's the way it works." He went back to his *Road & Track* magazine and told me to get out of his room before he told Pierre Letourneau, a French boy I'd worshipped since kindergarten, that I was in love with him.

A few weeks later Patty's mother came to the door in a see-through nightie and gold slippers even though it was only three o'clock in the afternoon. "You're not sick, are you, Mrs. Templeton?"

"Not sick, no, Diane," she said, pulling open the door partway. She slicked her hand through her hair, which wasn't wet but wasn't dry either. Through her pyjamas, her breasts seemed to heave as though the effort of talking was almost too much for her. "Can I help you with something?" she said.

I looked past her into the house. The curtains were drawn in the living room and the house had a sweet pleasant smell. "Are you baking?"

She smiled. "No, I'm not baking."

"I'm supposed to meet Patty," I said. "We're going to the Youth Club."

Mrs. Templeton nodded her head and her whole body swayed. She gestured for me to step a little closer. "It's Mr. Templeton," she whispered.

I stepped a little closer. "What about him?" I started to whisper back. Then Mr. Templeton appeared in the doorway. He was wearing a terry cloth bathrobe with his initials embossed on it—P.E.T. He grabbed Mrs. Templeton from behind and gave her bum a good squeeze.

"Bye bye, little girl," he said, even though he knew my name. Then he shut the door, and I heard Mrs. Templeton giggle.

A few seconds later Patty came out, favouring a paper cut on her right index finger. "Blood," she said, looking at her finger satisfactorily. "We're going to be surrounded by blood our entire lives, Diane, and there's nothing we can do about it." She stuck her finger in her mouth and sucked on it, saying, "We might as well get used to it now."

Patty told me the trick with the rubber was to keep it rolled up before you slip it on. She demonstrated in a corner booth at Miss Chinatown with the plastic wrapper from one of the hot towels they bring you at the end with the fortune cookies and the bill.

"It's a drag when this happens," Patty said. She held the rolled-up towel in the air above the table, then let it flop over, limp. It reminded me of Stanley. "Especially before you even start anything down there," she said. Patty helped herself to more noodles. Then she said, "Did you know that if you sneeze and have an orgasm at the same time, you die?" I shook my head. "It's true," she said. "Catherine told me the other night when I was helping her smooth depilatory cream on her bikini line."

Catherine was Patty's oldest sister and the one with the most dates, and according to Patty had to do her bikini line at least twice a week or she'd get itchy and have to scratch. "Can you imagine?" Patty gestured to a place under the table, and I looked away.

"Really?" I gulped, then I coughed to cover up the gulping sound in my throat. Mrs. Lee came over and asked me if anything was wrong. "No, I'm fine," I said, so she shuffled back over to her place near the all-you-can-eat buffet.

"What did you get?" I asked Patty on our way out. We squinted at each other in the sunlight with little slits for eyes. No matter what time of day it was outside, they dimmed the lights inside the restaurant so it was always night and you couldn't see what you were eating. We pretended to hear eggrolls meow, chow mein bark, and stuck to dishes like deep-fried noodles and fortune cookies.

"Good luck and prosperity are you for the asking?" Patty said.

"Happiness coming to those who are waiting," I said.

Every Saturday, Brother Maurice, who later quit the brotherhood to become an announcer at a strip club called "Girls, Girls, Girls" in Pensacola, Florida, ran another kind of club in the church basement that Patty and I went to. That afternoon on our way to the Youth Club, we interpreted the fortunes, deciphering the secret coded messages contained between the lines of red writing.

Reading my fortune, Patty figured second time's a charm. "Says so right here," she said. "Happiness coming, with Stanley McGoldbrick, to those—that's you, who are—have been—patiently, waiting."

She handed me her fortune. "Now do me," she said.

"Okay." I wracked my brain, but I just wasn't as clever as Patty was. "Good luck..." I said. Patty nodded her head eagerly. "Good luck...good luck and prosperity are *yours* for the asking." Patty pulled a face. "It's a typo, Patty," I said, but I could tell I'd disappointed her.

"That's okay," she said. "No, really that's okay."

A salt truck motored by us, spraying the boulevard with Safe-T-Salt. It was November and frosty. Earlier in the day, a snow shower had left the whole neighbourhood sparkling and the streets too slick to drive on. There was a thin layer of cracked ice over everything.

Patty looped her arm through mine as she sidestepped a pile of frozen dog poop. "Watch where you walk," she said. The last thing either of us wanted to do was to show up at the Youth Club smelling like dog poop. Then we walked the rest of the way to church without talking, our hands jammed deep into our pockets to keep them warm. Patty hummed something folksy—a hymn I didn't remember the title of— while I kept time with a hand tapping against my thigh.

Patty Templeton and I had been best friends since my seventh birthday when she swung a bathroom door into my nose at the Ponderosa Steak House and broke it. With perfect timing, Patty hammered on the cubicle door just as I was unlocking it and *whamo!* right in the kisser. Later when we were older and wiser, we called it Kismet and Destiny and Fortune, but at the time both nostrils bled for the better part of an hour, and I didn't even get to taste the horse-shaped ice-cream cake before Mum raced me out of the restaurant and home to bed, panic-stricken because I was beginning to look a little pasty.

At home, though, the bleeding stopped almost right away; my father thought I was out of danger.

"What do you think, Fred?" Mum asked him. They were still in love then; my father had not yet started disappearing for long stretches of time. The two of them stood at the foot of my bed looking at me as if I was good enough to eat. I was in new baby doll pyjamas, with my head tilted back against the headboard, listening to a *glug glug* sound coming from my throat. I was surrounded by birthday presents, most of them still wrapped.

By the time my father managed to say, "I think my birthday girl's looking a little better," I had my mouth open in what felt like a hiccup; but it wasn't a hiccup and I got barf all over the bed and the presents and me because, by then, I had simply swallowed too much steak *haché* and blood.

The Youth Club was supposed to be a club for teenagers, but by the time most of the kids in our parish grew into teenagers, they didn't want to join any club whose motto was "God's Club Is My Club, Is The Youth Club" run by a man who called himself Brother Maurice around adults, and Bro Moe around kids.

By 1977 Patty and Andy and Stanley and I were border-line—we were getting too old for the Youth Club, and even Brother Maurice knew it—but nobody wanted to be the first one to hurt Brother Maurice's feelings by dropping out. We went anyway. We didn't wear the T-shirts anymore though, and most Saturdays we moseyed in late, with cigarettes on our breath and scowls on our faces, if we bothered to mosey in at all.

At the club, the girls played board games, or sometimes Dodge Ball until someone got hurt. The boys sent pennies skimming across the linoleum, and the one closest to the wall won all the pennies. Brother Maurice, claiming to have had an addictive personality (drugs, alcohol, gambling, you name it) before cleaning up his act and joining the brother-hood, made them play with pennies instead of quarters because quarters tended to up the ante too much. One day after the club, he even confessed to me that he'd be hard-pressed to resist the temptation of all that silver glistening on the floor.

"The devil dances in an empty pocket," he said.

"Don't I know it," I said, humouring him.

My favourite game was Trouble, mostly because I liked popping the little dice trapped inside the bubble. I liked the size of the game, too, and the way all the pieces fit, one inside the other. Patty's favourite was Operation, even though Brother Maurice was always threatening to disconnect the buzzer and take the fun out of it. The buzzer got on his nerves and made him edgy.

In the game, the idea is to remove plastic pieces of the human body from inside these little cavities without touching the side with the tweezers; if you touch, the buzzer goes and a light flashes where the patient's heart is supposed to be. Patty had steady hands and never set off the buzzer, but I set off the buzzer almost all the time.

"Don't look now," Patty said to me that Saturday. She was in the middle of a delicate operation, hauling out the broken heart, and winning, and had a tidy pile of organs collected beside her. I had the wishbone though.

"What, what?" I said, careful not to look at anything but the thing I was looking at. But then Brother Maurice was standing beside me, and I could smell his sweet breath on my neck.

Patty set off the buzzer on purpose and Brother Maurice jerked forward. "Oh so close," she said, handing the tweezers to me.

"Hello girls," Brother Maurice said. He gritted his teeth at Patty and then placed his fingers on my shoulder and tapped them. Upstairs in the church, Madame Juneau was practising her scales on the electric organ, serenading us with one version of "Do Re Mi" after another.

Patty sang, "Do, Re, Mi, Fa, Sol," with a hand cupped over her mouth for the echo, until I joined in.

"Laa, Ti, Do."

"Have you seen Stanley McGoldbrick, Diane?" Brother Maurice interrupted. He leaned forward and pointed to the boys on the other side of the room. Stanley wasn't among them. I'd noticed.

"No," I answered quickly, guiltily. Since our disaster in Andy Hampton's basement I'd been avoiding him, though Stanley himself was anxious to give it another try. He'd called me up the week before, but I'd had my period then so I told Stanley to hold his horses even though Patty informed me— as if I didn't know—you could still do it then.

We Could Stay Here All Night

Patty had always been one step ahead of me. She got her first period when she was ten years old before she even knew what was happening to her; I got mine during the premiere of "Saturday Night Fever" in Surround Sound and I had to sneak in because I wasn't fourteen yet—I was thirteen, and had been waiting for three long years to catch up to Patty.

In the end though, I was disappointed that there wasn't very much blood. I'd expected it to gush. My old auntie, who was in her sixties and on my father's side of the family, claimed she still bled like a stuck pig every month, though my mother said she was lying, said there were women like Auntie Clare and Patty Templeton who simply had to talk about it every month, and then there were women like us. By us, she meant Granny, Mum, and me.

Back then I had to tiptoe out of the cinema during John Travolta's big dance contest scene and wait in the bathroom until the movie was over. Later when I told Patty what had happened, she said, "Congratulations" and gave me a bottle of Charlie like it was my birthday or something.

"Your turn," Patty said. Then the door opened, and Stanley blew in with Danny Chicarelli, a boy who'd once whispered "Masturbate me" in my ear during a provincial exam.

"There he is," I told Brother Maurice, blushing.

As Brother Maurice trundled off towards Stanley McGoldbrick and Danny Chicarelli, Patty warned me about the dangers of Spanish fly.

"What's that?" I asked her.

Patty said, "Don't you know what Spanish fly is?" I shook my head. Patty cleared her throat and swatted the air with the back of her hand. "For your information, Spanish fly is this stuff that guys will try and slip into your drink at parties."

"Stuff? What kind of stuff?" I said.

"It doesn't matter what kind of stuff, Diane. It's stuff-stuff. The point is, Spanish fly makes you really horny. Catherine got some slipped into her Coke at a party last weekend," she said. "Lucky for her, she had enough smarts to know what it was, get home, and lock herself in her bedroom until it wore off."

"Wow."

"That's what I thought," Patty said, and then she was quiet for a while.

There was a five o'clock Mass on Saturdays where Brother Maurice dished out Holy Communion. "See you later," he said to us. He shook a handful of pennies in my direction, winking.

Usually Brother Maurice shut down the club early. He needed time to get over to the friary, change out of his blue jeans and turtleneck and into his costume, before heading back to church. But that Saturday he was so happy to see us all, he couldn't contemplate kicking us out. He sang a few lines to me from "Peace Train" before heading out alone. He was such a push-over. He handed the keys to Stanley McGoldbrick and told him to lock up. "Can Bro Moe trust you?" Brother Maurice asked Stanley. Stanley was the oldest altar boy in our church and everybody trusted him.

"Yes, I believe he can," Stanley said, crossing himself.

After Brother Maurice disappeared up the back stairs, Stanley booted everyone out except for Patty and Andy and me. Then Stanley lit up. He smoked Colts. He offered one to me, then held out the pack to the other two.

"I love these," said Andy, lighting up. We stood around in a circle, puffing clouds of smoke, listening to the organ music grinding upstairs. At first I liked the taste of the Colt, and smacked my lips on its wine-tipped filter. But then the boozy grape flavour of the tip was gone, and it just tasted like a cigar.

Stanley grinned at me then and I saw a gap where one of his front teeth used to be. Patty saw it, too. She gasped.

"What happened to your tooth, Stanley?" I said then.

Stanley shrugged it off. "Fight."

"Who won?" Patty said and giggled. Stanley glared at Patty like he wanted to hit her. Then he told us the Colt fit in his gap perfectly, and maybe he wouldn't be wanting the prosthesis his mother was getting him fitted for after all.

"See?" Stanley said. He lifted up his lip and showed us the Colt sitting in the gap. Then he shifted the Colt so I could touch it. I reached my hand out towards him and ran my finger over the gap, feeling bumpy roots where the tooth used to be. Patty had a turn, too. Suddenly we were all so brave.

Stanley settled the Colt again, before sauntering away, all hip.

Before we split up into pairs, Patty whispered that all men's dinks were the same size. "It's a myth," she said, "That thing about them being different sizes. They're all exactly one hundred percent alike." Then Andy led Patty across the floor to the room where the Cub Scouts kept their star charts while I followed Stanley over to the coat check where Father Paul stored bingo cards, unblessed wafers and extra bottles of communion wine. He unlocked the door and we tiptoed in. The room had a nice fruity smell. I clicked the door shut.

"Leave it open," Stanley said.

I said, "What for?"

"The light," he said. "I want to see what I'm doing."

I opened the door partway; twilight from the windows along the back wall crept into the room. It was five o'clock.

At first Stanley didn't even try anything. We laid side by side on the hard linoleum, where the temperature was at least fifteen degrees cooler than it was in the air circulating above us, while Stanley sent smoke rings swirling. I told Stanley what Patty said. He scoffed. "She's a liar. Mine is two inches longer than Andy's already. What do you think about that?"

"You measured it?" I said. Then I butted out. Stanley finished the Colt and his hands slid up under my shirt and all over. With one hand he unhooked my bra. It snapped forward and bunched up under my chin like a pretty beige scarf. Then he walked his fingers down my stomach to the top button of my blue jeans.

"Okay," he said, like he was answering a question I'd just asked him. I took a deep breath, while Stanley struggled down below.

"Maybe it's the wrong size, Stanley," I volunteered after a few minutes.

"I didn't see a size on it," Stanley whispered, all-defensive like.

"Maybe you should relax then." I ran my hands through Stanley's hair like they did on late-night television.

"Relax?" Stanley gestured to the rubber, which he was wearing half-on, half-off. "Exactly how am I supposed to relax?"

I blew in Stanley's ear and could see my own breath. "Like this," I whispered back, using a deep throaty voice.

"Quit it, Diane," Stanley said, pushing me away from his ear. "You're making me too hot." Hot.

I thought about Patty and Andy then in the throes of passion in the Cub Scout closet stretched out on green felt, and imagined they weren't in the same sorry predicament that Stanley and I were in.

Stanley finally stuck it in for a few minutes, but when nothing happened he yanked it out again real quick.

"Not so fast, Stanley," I said. I wanted time to ache, to feel the little hurt my mother was talking about; but instead felt nothing, not even a pinch.

"This isn't right," said Stanley. He hauled off the rubber with a single tug and it made a snapping sound in his hand like an elastic band breaking. "Damn it all," he said.

I put my head back and spied through the open door. Along the back wall, I could make out pairs of legs hurrying by the windows, and purses swinging, late for church. The world was upside down.

New Women

Patty forgot to take her birth control pill yesterday morning. "That's twice this month," she tosses off with a giggle over breakfast. She pops two in her mouth, just to be safe, and rinses them down with orange juice. They look like the little white saccharine pills my mother used to drop one by one into her coffee before she found out saccharine caused cancer in laboratory animals. The Surgeon General's report on the ill effects of smoking was largely ignored, mind you. I wonder for a moment if the little white pills taste as sweet as they look.

"Do you know what that means?" she asks. I nod. Despite everything my mother and father did to keep the knowledge from me, I did know. I found out in the hallways of my Catholic high school.

I'm still not so sure Patty's being pregnant is such a good idea though, no matter how indifferent she appears to the news. So, in lieu of faking a phoney cheerfulness and pretending to congratulate her, I clasp my hands together and rock my arms back and forth. My clever mother and child symbolism is all in vain, however, as she is busy jamming a fork into my toaster to make it pop and has her back to me. I think she is taking unnecessary risks with her unborn child's health.

"Did you know you can have them home delivered now?" she says.

Well, of course you can, I think. They've been home delivering babies for decades. As a matter of fact, they were home delivering them before they began delivering them anywhere else.

"Sure," I reply. "Remember that book we read about midwifery? The one for our New Women class?" Patty and I are taking a correspondence course together entitled New Women. It was her idea. Anyway, if nothing else, the class has helped me realise the importance of celibacy. It seems I'd been adhering to the principles for a while anyway, however unwittingly, so I figured what the hell. Patty thinks I'm crazy.

"Midwifery?" she says. "Diane, what are you talking about?"

"Home deliveries," I say. Patty is obviously having some difficulty following our conversation. I think I had better slow down. She probably has a lot on her mind, what with the baby and all.

Suddenly she begins to laugh. Not giggling as usual, but convulsing with hysterical laughter. At my expense. I'm not certain this is good for the child either.

"You think...you actually think..." Peals of laughter echo through my kitchen. I consider asking for my sundress back.

The white one with the criss-cross straps on the sides that she likes so much. She won't be able to fit into it soon anyway.

"I'm not pregnant!" she shouts, composing herself. It's about time. "I'm talking about condoms. Condoms."

"Oh," I say, then, "Somebody actually home delivers condoms for a living?"

"I just meant that Mark and I would have to use condoms for the rest of the month so I don't get pregnant, that's all." *Well*, I think, *why tell me? Why tell me?*

Patty's a great girl. Or rather, a great New Woman. She is the only friend I have who can as easily talk about sex as have it. She has *The Joy of Sex*—the full-colour edition—on her living room bookshelf. I've got *Everything You've Always Wanted to Know About Sex, But Were Afraid to Ask* at the back of my closet under my ski boots, and nobody knows it's there. Not even Patty. It reads more like a step by step introduction to cooking than anything else. Happily, I'm a good cook. Or at least I've had no complaints recently. No steady boyfriends, but no complaints either.

"Assertiveness," I say. It's exam time and Patty and I are actively preparing for our upcoming New Women final. It would be unbearable to flunk out as New Women. We're staging a mock exam in her living room. I want a four word definition for assertiveness.

"Five...six...seven...eight. Not taking any bullshit from men," she answers. She is prone on the carpet with little mauve weights strapped to her ankles, doing leg lifts. Sexually, she tells me, she's more flexible this way. Before strapping on the weights, she completed two sets of twenty pelvic tilts.

"That's six words." The directions suggested brevity; use as few words as possible. Patty wanted to use six in the first place, but I thought three would be plenty. So, we compromised. That's what friendship's all about.

"Five...six...seven...eight. Then how 'bout not taking any bullshit, period. The men-bit is implied anyway."

"Okay." I write down her definition. When we finish, we're going to correct each other's papers using blood-red, felt-tipped markers.

"Aggression." I've been mixing up the A's to try and throw her off.

"Misplaced hostility toward women when it's men you're really mad at."

"That's eleven, Patty. Four words, remember?" She nods her head. It's a good answer though. New Women advocate sticking together.

"Misplaced hostility toward women then. I think the word misplaced says it all. Don't you?"

"You're probably right." I jot down her answer. I might not get the chance to cover her page in red after all. As far as I can tell, she's doing pretty well.

"Avoidance," I say. This is one of her favourites. She's planning on doing her term paper on avoidance. I'm doing mine on abstinence.

"Dodging the real problem," she says. "Men are good at this," she adds. And I just have to hand it to her. She knows exactly what she's talking about from real-life experience. A few weeks ago, she videotaped an oral presentation about this guy she used to see, and then mailed it off to other New Women. She simply set the self-timer on the video camera at ninety minutes and away she went. It was really something. Frank, honest and entertaining. I'm camera-shy myself, so I opted to take a self-defense workshop instead of mailing an oral presentation to the class. That's just one of the nice things about the course. New Women have options.

"That'd be Mark," she says with a grin. Then she rolls onto her other side and begins again.

Mark comes in with a newspaper under his arm. Apparently, he has key privileges to her apartment. I can't remember what the books say about key privileges.

"Hi girls," he smiles. Patty freezes—her left leg slicing through the air to the floor. It lands with a thud.

"We're New Women," she says breathlessly. They're five pound weights.

"New Women," he corrects himself. And I figure it's time to go. It is getting late.

"How many times have I told you not to call us girls? It's derogatory." She shakes her head while pulling herself into a lotus position. "Diane thinks it's derogatory too. Don't you?"

I decline to comment. So much for all for one and one for all.

"And how many times have I asked you not to triangle?" Mark says. And while I'm not too sure I know exactly what Mark means, I sense it has something to do with me.

"I'm not," Patty insists. "I was just looking for an objective third party. An impartial observer."

"Diane's not objective or impartial," he says, his voice rising an octave or so and then cracking. "She's your best friend and she's a New Woman!" I slowly untuck my legs and begin to ease myself out of the chair I've been sitting on. I am hoping they won't notice my swift departure. From between the pages of the New Women study guide though, Patty's copy of *The Joy of Sex* crashes to the floor. I'd forgotten it was hidden there.

Patty stares at the book and then at me.

"It's research for my term paper," I explain lamely. I'd hate to have her think I wasn't paying attention. Between questions, I was merely trying to recall precisely what it is I've been abstaining from.

"Sit down," Patty says to me. "We're not through yet." I sit and retrieve the questionnaire from the floor. The next word on the list is anxiety. I need a four word definition for anxiety. Anybody?

Patty sets up an interview for us with an exotic dancer named Eve. Before we can receive final accreditation, we have to document the continuing oppression of women in the eighties. It's the single requirement we have left to fulfil before writing the exam and being certified New Women. It's almost like finally being inducted into a secret club after months of initiation tests.

"Think of it as doing field work," Patty says to reassure me. I am feeling a little apprehensive about our appointment. I have never met an exotic dancer before. I don't know what to say.

As we head out the door, Patty receives a telephone call from one of the other women in the New Women class. She's forming a fringe group and breaking away from what she refers to as the 'inherent sexism in the word Women'. The splinter group is called "Wo" (pronounced woe). She wants Patty to drop New Women and join up with Wo. Patty would be a real addition, the woman says. There are already three of them.

"What do you think?" she asks me after hanging up. I can tell she's pleased with the invitation. Patty and her video have evidently garnered quite a reputation over the past few weeks.

"I don't know," I reply. And I mean it. The whole thing may well be getting out of hand. A fringe group? It sounds radical.

"It might be fun," she says.

"A group called Wo?" I wonder aloud. And then she giggles. It is pretty funny when you think about it.

We arrive at Foxy's just in time to catch Eve's act. It's quite a complicated number. Tightly choreographed, I imagine. When she's finished, Patty waves her over to our table.

"Nice snake," I say because I can't think of anything else. Patty kicks me under the table before furiously grabbing

Eve's hand and shaking it. And I know I am supposed to follow Patty's lead in all this, but I can't. I am unable to wrench my eyes from Eve's right breast long enough to find her hand. She has her name tattooed on it in red ink above the tassel. Ouch.

"Did you know that a man with no high school degree, not even a diploma of any kind, earns more money than a woman with a university degree?" Patty begins. Eve shakes her head no. Her tassels swing a little to the left. "And that for every dollar a man earns, a woman earns sixty-two cents? Sixty-two cents!" she says, repeating herself for emphasis. Eve shakes her head again as the snake begins to coil itself around her wrist. "Women are nowhere near equality!" Patty shouts. I am slightly taken aback. And I have to wonder if Patty couldn't be a bit more subtle in her approach. "Women still need—"

"Aren't you with the newspaper?" Eve interrupts. "I thought you told me over the telephone you were with the paper?" I look over at Patty. She simply shrugs. She had to tell her something, I suppose in Patty's defense.

"I guess that's that," I say. "Can we go now?"

"Not yet," Patty says. "We still have to hand out the leaflets we prepared. Here, you take half the pile and start over there."

Eventually we are asked to leave on account of we are distracting the dancers and bothering the patrons. Patty stands firm. She wants to finish handing out the leaflets before going anywhere. I'd just as soon leave. The in-house response to our question and answer brochure was dismal anyway. One guy immediately crumpled it into a paper ball and threw it back at me. He didn't even read it. Another guy folded it into a miniature airplane and tried to taxi onto the stage while the dancers squealed a mixture of delight and disgust. But at least he glanced at it first.

"Ladies, please," the doorman urges.

"New Women!" Patty screams at him. "We're New Women! Why can't anybody see that?!"

The doorman scoops Patty up under his arm and carries her over to the door. He deposits her under the neon exit sign. I follow them, quickly distributing the remaining leaflets along the way. I give two, sometimes three, brochures to a table.

Outside Patty asks me my opinion of Eve. We are standing under the club's flashing marquee. It's not neon, like inside. It's really just a string of light bulbs, the kind used on Christmas trees. It's supposed to spell out Foxy's, I guess, but most of the bulbs are burnt out or the sockets are empty. It flashes FO.

My opinion of Eve? Patty's taking copious notes for the class and writing them down in a little pad with "I Love Cooking" on the front flap.

"She didn't look oppressed," I say. "She looked...cold."

Patty nods her head in agreement and writes down my opinion in the column under my name. So far she's written "Stalwart in the face of opposition." I'm flattered.

On Tuesday Patty calls me up to tell me she's passed the New Women exam with flying colours. I'm not surprised. She's even been asked to conduct a series of on-going development workshops for the New Women graduates. It's the first time she'll be face to face with dozens of other New Women.

"We still have to stick together," she reminds me. "It doesn't matter that the actual course is over. New Women continue to need support. Solidarity forever!" she shouts into the telephone receiver. I notice she's been shouting a lot lately. First at that stripper and now at me.

I try to act surprised at her news, but I'm not. I have already been encouraged to enrol in her workshops by the founder of New Women. She said it would be in my best interests to take as many workshops as possible, and not just the ones Patty will be teaching, if I seriously intend to remain a New Woman. I was not aware that my New Woman status could be revoked, but I've decided to take two courses for starters.

I tell Patty I'm happy for her and that I'll be in one of her workshops as a New Woman grad. She congratulates me for passing the exam. I don't tell her I barely scraped by.

The first course is an intensive three-day seminar called "Gender Panic." TBA was written under the course description, so I have no idea what to expect from this one. The title leads me to believe that there might be men in it though, or at least a male lecturer or guest or something. I hope so. With the exception of Patty's boyfriend, Mark, I haven't seen a man in months. Patty admires me for this. She thinks I'm brave.

I've already pre-registered for her "It Isn't Fair" workshop, although she doesn't know it yet. Our first class together is in one weeks' time. I can hardly wait. The course description says the group will learn the methodology behind primal scream therapy and, by the end of six weeks, will be able to properly employ a number of associated techniques in their individual lives.

I suppose then that I'm going to learn how to scream. Really scream. That's probably what Patty's been shouting about for the past couple of weeks.

Mount of Venus

When I was fourteen years old, my father put all he cared about in the trunk of his white Impala and drove as far away from my mother and brother and me as he could get. It was 1976 and he went to British Columbia to work scheduled maintenances in oil refineries and pulp and paper mills, and never came back.

"It was more complicated than that," my mother told me later. She was sitting in front of an overflowing ashtray, still hanging on to the telephone receiver even though the caller, a woman who was looking for my father, had long since hung up. "The future," she said, "looked complicated." I nodded, still pretending to understand my father's obsession with the future. All our lives, while my mother had put her faith in God, and let the parish priest instruct my brother Wayne and me how to do the same thing, my father had looked to his life line, which he saw as long and solid, and the luck lines that rose from the hump on his hand known as the Mount of Venus.

"God, Diane," my mother said, gripping my arm with knuckles going white. "What am I going to do now?" She dropped her head into her hands, confirming what I'd already suspected: she still loved him.

I took the receiver from my mother, and gently placed it back in its cradle. It was a Thursday morning in June. I looked out the window at our neighbour's blue and white *fleur-de-lys* sailing in the breeze. I thought about my father, the angle of his chin, and the way his eyelids moved in sleep.

The last time I saw my father, he was standing outside the Seabus station on Vancouver's North Shore where the Capilano River pours into the Burrard Inlet. I was seventeen, I'd just graduated from high school, barely, and had travelled across country by Greyhound to see him, against my mother's better judgement.

"What if he doesn't want to see you, Diane? Have you thought about that? He probably has a new future which has nothing to do with you, me, or your brother." My mother and father had not seen each other in the years since he left, but she'd spoken to him over the telephone in late night calls he'd always made collect and full of liquor.

"Maybe he's dying to see me," I said, hopefully.

"Maybe the last thing he wants is the family he deserted looking him up."

"He hardly deserted us, Mum," I said, which wasn't true at all. He had deserted us, time and time again. When I was six years old, in the middle of the night he moved across town to the music teacher's house where he'd already been keeping some of his clothes for the better part of a year; then a few years later, after losing his shirt in a bad business venture with his brother, my father moved to a small town in northern Quebec where he fell in love with a French woman who took off her clothes for a living. We'd lived like this for years.

"Who are you to go mucking around in other people's lives?" my mother asked me.

"His daughter," I said. My mother nodded. She believed I was my father's daughter. Then Ramon came in through the back door, reeking of skin bracer, and my mother said, "You're late."

My father was scanning the crowd as everyone on the bus disembarked. He spotted me right away. "You've got your mother's eyes," he said right off. Then, "I don't know what she's doing for a pair these days." He swatted the air with the back of his hand, still killing himself laughing over his own jokes, before reaching out and pulling me to him in an awkward embrace.

"Ha ha," I said, holding him to me. He was thinner than I remembered, shorter somehow. Next year he would turn fifty.

"Where to?" he said, letting go first.

I shook my head. I'd just arrived. I hadn't been anywhere, except the youth hostel to stash my bags. I said, "Anywhere is good."

On our way through the market, vendors, mostly women, said hello to him. My father glanced over his left shoulder, as if he was afraid of being followed. "So what did you want to see me for?" he called out. Passing a fruit stand, he helped himself to a too-ripe banana. I shrugged. I wasn't sure myself. "Didn't your mother and Raoul warn you about me?"

"Ramon," I said. Ramon was the real estate salesman who'd swept my mother off her feet a few years earlier.

"All the drinking?" he said, almost boasting. "The women? The gambling?"

"They warned me already," I said, and they had.

My father took me to a waterfront bar made out to look like a tugboat. I looked out a porthole over the water to the place I'd just come from. A dirty seagull swooped past.

The waitress in the bar knew my father, too. "Sit anywhere, Freddy," she said. My father moved us over to a table against the far wall, then said he'd be right back. I watched as he walked off in the direction of the bathrooms we'd passed on the way in. Above my head, rubber lobsters dangled and plastic starfish clutched nylon netting.

He brought the waitress back to the table with him, holding her snugly around the waist. "Anything you want, sweetheart," he told me. "Sky's the limit." He threw a fifty dollar bill on the table.

I considered this. "Beer?" I said. I was underage— seventeen—and looked it. My father shook his head. "Bring her a beer, Doris." Then he put his hands on the table, palms up. We shared a forked life line, that much I remembered, and a pointed mercury finger—the baby—signalling restlessness.

When my father ordered coffee, I wanted to change my order, call Doris back, and say two coffees. Black. I didn't want a beer. It was too early for beer. But I didn't say a word, and when the beer came, I gulped it down too quickly.

"I brought photos," I said.

I held out one of me and Wayne and Mum all together the Christmas before. We are standing around an artificial tree early Christmas morning, smiling at Ramon who is behind the camera pulling faces at us. My father stared closely at the photograph, then held it up at an angle to catch a shaft of light streaming in through the porthole. He studied my mother's handwriting on the back. Then he put it down on the table near his coffee cup and said, "Your mother was always a sucker for tinsel."

"Tinsel?"

"Do you remember the Christmas she made us hang each strand individually? No throwing?"

I said I remembered, and I did, but it was the same thing we did every year whether he'd been there or not. He asked how things were in "La Belle Province." He asked after our dog, a twelve year-old terrier that went crazy soon after he left and had to be put down. He asked about my brother. "Does he still hate me?" my father wondered.

"No," I said, but the expression on his face told me he knew I was lying.

"Is he famous yet?" I shook my head. My father remembered Wayne's boyhood dreams of being a hockey player for the Montreal Canadiens and knew nothing of his current dream to get into the real estate business.

"He doesn't even skate anymore," I said.

"Does he live with you and your mother and Ralph still?"

"Ramon," I said. Across the table, my father pushed his shirt sleeves up over his forearms and revealed a tattoo. It had a picture of an anchor on it in blue ink and the words "Remember Pearl Harbour" in block letters. I counted backwards. My father had been four years old when Pearl Harbour was attacked.

I said, "Wayne lives in Toronto. He's at university, studying business." A hint of pride crept into my voice, but my father didn't notice. He was too busy picking at a scab on his forearm near the tattoo.

When there was a pause in the conversation and I was beginning to think I'd found what I was looking for, he asked me if I liked salmon. I said it was okay.

"Have you had west coast salmon? I bet you haven't. Say, I know what," he said suddenly. He slapped the table with his hand, spilling coffee on the photograph. "We'll go fishing."

"I don't want to go fishing," I told him. He looked at me then with a weird expression on his face, so I said, "I'm not dressed for fishing."

"You're fine," he said. "Tell you what. We'll go back to my place, and Rosalie will lend you something to wear. She's your size."

I wanted to ask him who Rosalie was, but suddenly I wondered what he thought of me coming all this way to visit.

"Rosalie's the lady I live with now," he volunteered. "I live in a park, you know." He gestured out the porthole to a clump of dying trees. I looked out the window in the direction of his hand. "Just over there."

"Diane?" he said, standing up. "Let's go fishing."

I followed my father along railway lines, past the BC Rail Terminal, past the Vancouver Wharves, until we reached a trailer park under the Lion's Gate Bridge where Rosalie reclined in a strappy chaise lounge holding an out-of-date *Time* magazine in her hands. She was a big woman, not my size at all, with strong hands and a long black ponytail that hung down the back of her neck like a thick rope.

"You look like your father," Rosalie said to me, taking me by the hand. We went into the trailer together while my father waited outside, dragging the toes of his shoes in the gravel. The trailer was run-down, slanted on the side so that in one corner, a small pile of junk had accumulated: a tennis ball, a pop bottle, several pennies. With the exception of a few fading photographs pinned up over a small sink, the place had the look and feel of an old hotel, a room that was occupied only for short periods of time, and was currently vacant.

I stood at the sink and stared at the photographs as Rosalie rummaged through a damp box of clothing for something my size. There was a cheesecake snapshot of my mother in her bathing suit, taken back in her swimming days before I was born, and there was one of my brother and me taken one Halloween: I am some kind of mushroom and my brother looks like a drunk.

"You were a cute kid," Rosalie said, watching me. She

lent me an old pair of jeans and a wool sweater with holes in the elbows. She told me she'd knitted it herself. "You'll need these, too," she said, handing me a pair of rubber boots.

As I changed, Rosalie sat on the edge of the bed. She studied her nails, scraping off what was left of the pink polish. "Rosalie?" I said. She looked up. "Does my father ever talk about the future?"

"The future?" she repeated. "No, I can't say that he does." I nodded, pulling on Rosalie's jeans. "I've heard all about the past though," she said quietly. Then my father knocked on the trailer door and said, "What's taking you girls so long? The fish won't be running forever."

We stood on one side of the Capilano River.

"Here's the spot," my father said. Then he told me to wait for him while he continued a few metres upriver. He disappeared into a stand of blackberry bushes. I sat down on the rocks and pulled my knees into my chest and hugged them. Suddenly, more than anything, I wanted to go home to Montreal, to my mother and Ramon.

My father returned with an old Safeway shopping cart that he wheeled over the rocks past the place where I was sitting. Where the river grew narrow, he laid the shopping cart down on its side, half-immersed in water. Then he sat back on his heels near the water's edge and waited. I stayed where I was, watching him.

One by one, the salmon running upriver swam into the shopping cart and were trapped. My father grinned as the fish flew into the cart, then he called out that we'd caught enough. It took all of forty minutes. He stepped over the rocks to the cart, then called my name.

"Diane," he said. "This is where you come in." I leapt up, suddenly anxious to be useful. He pointed to the cart and the fish trapped there. "Help me right this," he said.

I knelt next to him, with the sleeves of Rosalie's Cowichan sweater dipping into the frigid water, and helped him hoist the shopping cart upright. It was full of squirming silver fish, and it was all wrong, but I helped him anyway.

"That's my kind of fishing," my father said.

It took the two of us to push the cart over the rocks back to the trailer park. The wheels, rusty from sitting in the river for years, squealed. Once the wheels were clear of the rocks and were again squealing along the dirt path, I took over the job of pushing the cart alone while my father rooted around in the basket. He concentrated on pulling out the smaller fish and tossing them over his shoulder. "Small fry," he said. When he was satisfied that he had rid the basket of the smaller fish, he set about collecting the largest fish, chinook, and placing them in the part of the cart that I remembered sitting in as a child.

When we got back to the trailer park, Rosalie was gone. "She comes and goes," he said by way of explanation.

As I changed into my own clothes, my father called into the trailer, "I'll wrap these in aluminium foil for you, Diane."

"I don't want the salmon, Dad," I said, opening the door

and stepping down onto the gravel. He was standing in front of the picnic table gutting the largest fish we'd caught. It was the first time I'd called him Dad, but whether or not he noticed, I didn't know.

"Take the fish," he said.

We hugged, but as I began to pull away, he leaned suddenly forward and kissed me on both cheeks. "That's the way the French do it, isn't it?" he asked.

"Thanks for this," I said, holding up the fish. He smiled, rolling back and forth on the balls of his feet like a nervous date. Up close, I saw the nicks on his skin where he had cut himself shaving, trying to make a good impression. As I walked away, I thought I saw him looking into the palm of his hand. But then he coughed again and I realised that he was only looking at what he'd brought up before wiping his hand along a shirt sleeve.

Vermont

On the way home, coming back from the movie theatre in the mall on 41st Avenue, the car stalls somewhere near Granville Street. The motor quits and we coast. Steven turns the engine over, but nothing happens. It doesn't gag, or cough, or sputter to life, it simply clicks. I reach out and put my hand on Steven's thigh. Through his jeans I can feel the outline of his empty left front pocket, and I realize that I've never known how far down the pockets in a pair of Levis hang. I mark the inches with a baby finger bent at the knuckle that I've determined to be an exact inch and think again how nice it is to never have to be without an inch. When the four inches strike me as really short, I measure the distance again, my finger blindly tapping along his thigh, while he turns over the engine and curses.

We coast until the road starts curving up and the car starts rolling down.

"Stop measuring things!" he yells at me, suddenly jamming the car into P and getting out the driver's side. The door slams shut and everything seems very quiet all of a sudden.

With my scarf, I wipe a hole in the condensation and watch Steven make his way around to the front of the car. He fiddles with something about two inches under the hood, and for a minute the expression on his face is anxious. Then he pulls open the hood and props it up and I can't see him any-more. Sitting there, I blow on my hands and imagine we've broken down on a deserted stretch of road in the middle of Vermont or somewhere next to a cozy motel with an ice machine and free colour TV. And when Steven can't get the car going he opens the passenger door, holds out his hand, and says something like, "Looks like we have to spend the night, honey." And honey sounds sweet and deep and sincere in the cool Vermont air.

But then Steven raps on the windshield and accidentally hits his knuckle on the windshield wiper. He curses and shakes his hand and it reminds me of the time he burnt his hand on my iron after I told him to iron his own goddamned shirt. Then I'm back from Vermont and I'm in Vancouver and the car is dead on an incline in the middle of 41st Avenue and the parking brake hasn't worked since June.

"Are you merely going to sit there?" he shouts through the windshield, his face taking up the entire space I've just cleared for myself. For a moment, I look out at him, turning the word over and over in my mind, making it sound like honey. Soon his, "Are you merely going to sit there?" becomes my, "Are you, honey, going to sit there?" I open the door and gingerly step out onto the slick, black road. A star shines high up in the sky. On his side of the car, a station wagon with a bumper sticker that says *I'd Rather Be Sailing* swerves to avoid him and when he waves apologetically at the driver, the driver honks his horn twice and the baby in the car seat facing backwards gives Steven the finger.

"Fuck you, Buddy!" he yells, then he turns to me and says, "Look," so I squint in the dark but that's not what he means. "Would you please just stand still and hold the flashlight steady?" His voice borders on testy. I nod and stand in the shadow his back makes, holding the flashlight over his shoulder, measuring the distance between us.

I'm standing still and silent beside him, holding the light steady, until a single thread from my scarf starts tickling the inside of my nose. The light flashes into his eyes, then up his nose, then back under the hood, and the car slowly starts to roll down the hill.

A man and his dog come out of a house somewhere on 41st and a door bangs shut. The man sees me and smiles, so I wave. Then he sees Steven, and he can't ignore him as he chases, cursing, after the car.

"Here," the man says, handing me a leash that reminds me of the chain link fence surrounding our yard in Montreal. "He's a nice dog," he says, sprinting after Steven. "Big, but nice."

I stand there in the middle of the road saying quiet things like, "hello there" to the dog, watching the two of them chase after the car, when the nice dog places his nose in my crotch and sighs. It tickles at first, but then I can feel the damp imprint his nose leaves on my pants, and it's only cold and uncomfortable.

Steven, and the man who shouts out that his name is
Buck, manage to slow the car down, but it still rolls a little. I
feel awkward and helpless with Buck's dog's nose firmly
between my legs, so I try saying dog things like, "Sit pretty"
and, "Heel" and, "Stay" and, "Lie down," but when nothing
seems to work I decide that maybe Buck's dog is deaf. I
consider a few hand signals that the dog might know, but
give up when I realize that the dog probably can't see anything except the folds my pants make when they're bunched
up at the crotch.

When Steven and Buck reach the top of the hill, they're
both out of breath and sweaty. Buck says something about
not going anywhere tonight and Steven agrees and they start
talking about distributor caps and solenoid switches and Die
Hard batteries and the next thing you know, we're sitting
around the television in Buck's family room, drinking rum
and Cokes and watching "The Tonight Show" with David
Brenner sitting in for Johnny. I remark that I wish they'd let
Ed do it sometimes and Buck says that he and I must be a lot
alike because he's been thinking along those same lines for
some time now.

Buck's wife is the only one drinking straight rum, and I
watch her delicately tip back her sherry glass, sip, and sigh.
And I don't know how pleased she is when Buck suggests we
spend the night, but I do notice her lips on the sherry glass
for what seems like a long time.

"Oh Buck, we couldn't impose," Steven says and I'm
quick to shake my head and agree. When the dog sees me
doing this, he leaps into my lap, circles it once, then settles

down. Buck says something like "Down, Roger," but Roger doesn't move.

"We insist, kids," Buck says, looking over at his wife. "Right, Dear?" When he invited us inside, and we were still standing in the porch, Buck told us quietly that his wife's name really is Dear, but it's probably short for something.

"Shore," she says.

"No," I say, "We can catch a bus on Granville Street no problem."

"Not at this hour, honey-bunny," Buck says, referring to his digital wristwatch that has already beeped twice since we've been here.

Steven smiles at me from the La-Z-y Boy he's settled into, and for the first time since we arrived I notice his hand toying with the mahogany lever on the side. Next to it, there is a leather pouch stuffed with this week's *TV Times* and a tattered copy of *The Great Big Crossword Puzzle Book*. I wonder how long it will be before he swings back the lever and launches himself into a reclining position. He looks comfortable and right at home among Buck and Dear's black velvet wall hangings and Playboy Club beer mugs and miscellaneous volumes of the *Encyclopaedia Brittanica*. I sip my drink, watching him carefully, and realise that the Coke part of my rum and Coke has gone flat.

"We could take a cab," I say, but Buck tells me not to be silly.

"We got plenty a room," Buck says. "Besides, it'll be fun. Tomorrow's Saturday, we can all have...what's it called again, that cross between breakfast and lunch?"

"Brunch!" Steven shouts, swinging the lever back and startling Dear a little. She swallows the rest of her rum in one gulp without meaning to and coughs.

"Brunch. That's it. Right, Dear?" His wife says "shore" again, and turns up the corners of her mouth in what might be a smile, so I smile back at her. She begins to cry, and I don't know if it's Steven's fault or mine.

"Dear?" Buck says. Steven says something and I cross and uncross my legs and arms a few times. Dear gets up and makes for the stairs.

"Are you all right, Dear?" Buck calls out to her.

"Shore," she says, heading up the stairs without a second glance.

Steven says, "Is she..."

"Don't pay any attention to her. Dear's having a rough time of it," Buck says quietly.

Steven leans forward and the green leather he's sitting on squeaks and makes a funny sound. Buck leans forward, too, and they speak to each other in hushed voices like they're sharing an important secret.

"It's what I told you. It's Dutch," he says, and Steven nods his head sympathetically. I feel left out, wondering what went on at the bottom of the hill, until Buck sees me looking at him and explains that Dutch is his son.

"He disappeared," Buck whispers. "Late one night on a deserted road outside Moosejaw, he disappeared just like that." He snaps his fingers. "The police found his truck by the side of the road the next day, but Dutch was gone. Roger and the hogs were there, but Dutch was gone."

On television, David Brenner tells a joke that falls flat and David and Ed look at each other awkwardly and Steven and I look at David and Ed. Buck looks towards the stairs.

"It's like he drove right into one of those Bermuda triangles," he says suddenly.

When Doc strikes up the orchestra, "The Tonight Show" theme song comes on, and Buck switches off the set from a panel of colour-coded controls near his left hand.

"That thing you're setting on folds out into a couch," he says to me. "It's all made up. That's where Dutch used to sleep when he came through town." Steven smiles and thanks Buck. I say thanks, too.

"Boy, Rog certainly seems to like you," Buck says, pulling himself up and pointing to the dog in my lap. "Maybe he should sleep down here with you." I ask Buck if he's serious. He laughs and says, "Maybe not." Then, "Come on, Rog." Roger doesn't budge though, not with me pushing from behind or Steven pulling from in front. And I can't get up because Rog has cut off the circulation in my legs and they've fallen asleep. So I say never mind, Roger can sleep with me.

"Do you play bridge?" Buck asks on his way upstairs. I can only make out his feet on the stairs when he asks us.

I say "no" and Steven says "a little" at the same time. Buck's red plaid slippers suddenly stop and he seems to consider this as he shifts his weight from one foot to the other.

"That's great. I guess," he says, and then, "'Night, kids."

With a switch at the top of the stairs, Buck plunges us

into darkness. And now the only light in the room comes from the red and white Molson Canadian clock over the bar. It hums a little and gives off a strange reddish light that makes me think about shipwrecks and sailors' warnings. Steven says something about the kindness of strangers and I feel sad wondering what happened to Dutch. Then Steven offers to pull out the couch with me and Roger still on it. Roger falls off my lap and hits the floor with a thud, but doesn't wake up. The bed folds out over him, but I make sure a bed leg hasn't gored him before we sit down. In the couch, we find one of Roger's bones hidden between the cushions and before I slip under the covers I put Roger's bone beside him in case he wants it when he wakes up. When I look at him, his body starts to tremble a little. Steven sprawls out across the bed and hangs his head over the side to have a look.

"What's the matter with him?" I ask softly because I don't want him to wake up.

"It's just a dream," Steven says and rolls back.

"What do you suppose Roger dreams about?" I ask, but Steven doesn't answer.

"Cats? Do you suppose he dreams about cats?" Steven says no, he doesn't suppose Roger dreams about cats.

"What do you dream about?" he asks me. I shrug my shoulders and start measuring the arm of the couch with my inch.

"You, I guess," I say.

"Measuring," he says, "You dream about measuring."

"I do not," I say. "I dream about you."

"He's probably dreaming about other dogs then," he says

as if my answer has somehow helped him come up with his own.

Upstairs, someone's footsteps cross the floor, stop, and then cross back. Then they cross again, stop, and cross back. This goes on for a while, but I can't decide if the footsteps belong to Buck or Dear. They sound too heavy to belong to either of them. I reach under the covers for Steven, but he's got his back to me already and his arms stretched out in front of him. I roll over and face the Molson's clock. I'd really like to hear him tell me he loves me. I'd like those words to come out of his mouth as fast as a hiccup. And I want not to hear him, not clearly anyway, so he has to say them again, slowly, but his voice will crack this time, so I'll say, "What? I can't hear you." And when he says those words again, an ambulance will go by somewhere outside and the words will be muffled by the siren, so I'll say, "Sorry?" Until he'll finally get so frustrated he'll shout the words at me so loudly Buck or whoever's pacing up there will call down to ask, "What's up?"

But he doesn't, and I fall asleep to the sound of footsteps crossing the floor above us.

The Broom Closet

After my father's funeral, the entire family gets invited over to my grandmother's apartment to drink Chivas. It's a one-bedroom she shares with another widow in a high-rise building in downtown Montreal.

I go with my brother Wayne and our Uncle Lenny in my father's old white Impala which still smells like the cheap cigars he had started smoking. Frank gets invited along, too, because Uncle Lenny thinks he looks like a friend of my father's.

"So, are you interested in the magic business?" asks Uncle Lenny, sizing Frank up. He slips Frank a business card with the name of the company he owns embossed on it in fancy green script. "We'll talk later, Frankie," Uncle Lenny says. He rummages through the pockets of his pale blue suit for my father's car keys on the ring with one of my mother's swimming medals.

Frank fondles the card between long fingers, then slides into the back seat next to me. He puts a tender hand on my bare knee and leaves it there. Up front, my brother frowns at us in the rear view mirror. Frank and Uncle Lenny are about the same age.

Uncle Lenny turns the engine over once, then twice. On the third try, it catches, rumbles to life.

"Go easy, Len," Wayne says over the radio. "Watch you don't flood it."

"Len?" Uncle Lenny says. "What happened to Uncle Len?" Wayne shrugs his shoulders. He is hunched up in the front seat, leaning against the door. "Eh?" says Uncle Lenny.

"I don't know," Wayne says. Back in the seventies when we were growing up, Wayne started calling our father by his first name, too, after he'd come home from northern Quebec where he'd been working as a boiler maker, which had been his trade before Uncle Lenny sold the magic show to the CBC. "Welcome back, Fred," my brother had said. He was ten years old; I was eight. After that it was always Fred this, Fred that, but our father hadn't stuck around long enough to mind.

"Out of respect," Uncle Lenny says now, "I'd like you to say Uncle."

"Uncle," says Wayne, then Uncle Lenny steers us out of the church parking lot in the shadow of a black limousine. In the limousine, my mother sits smoking menthol cigarettes between my two grandmothers who do not get along. Auntie Clare is up front next to the driver whose name is Jean-Pierre.

We Could Stay Here All Night

✧

I was early for the funeral, so I stood outside the church in a bush of dying azaleas and watched the mourners arrive while Frank butted out cigarettes in a planter at the feet of the Virgin. At my mother's request, Father Paul, over eighty and no longer practicing, had taken a Greyhound bus up north from the New Jersey seashore.

"Father Paul," I said, but as I climbed the stairs to where he'd been propped up against the stained glass doors, it was obvious that he did not recognize me. Another priest, younger, hipper, obviously gay, introduced us.

"This is Fred Wilkinson's daughter, Diane," the priest said.

"Fred who?" Father Paul shouted.

My brother drove in from Ontario, where he'd moved years before when he realized his command of the French language would never be good enough.

"Hi Wayne," I said.

"Holy fuck. That's some get-up," Wayne said, referring to the granola look I'd been cultivating in British Columbia where I'd moved a few years earlier. "I wouldn't have recognized you." We hugged quickly, then separated to stand awkwardly looking at our feet. "Does this place ever bring back memories," he said.

"Brownies," I said.

"Beavers," he said. "Cubs, Boy Scouts."

I smiled. "Stanley McGoldbrick and I doing it in the coat check."

"Feeling up the French girls from the convent," he said.

Then our mother showed up with my two grandmothers and my father's elderly sister. She blew kisses in our direction, ushering us inside.

During the service, Father Paul nodded off during Uncle Lenny's eulogy and the altar boy had to nudge him awake. Gram wept for her favourite son, and next to me, Frank sobbed into a handkerchief. The rest of us remained dry-eyed.

At Gram's place Frank sits in the same upholstered chair, probably trying to stay as innocuous as possible, and nurses the drink my grandmother shoved into his hand when we first arrived. He looks worn out and wrinkled and he's still wearing the same grey pinstriped suit he was wearing on the airplane. I stand watching him from behind my old auntie's fox, but when he looks my way I pretend to be admiring it.

"Is this real, Auntie Clare?" I say. She cocks her head in my direction, which is good because it makes us look like we're really having a conversation together, and then shouts, "What?"

"Is this..." And then I stop because I can't ask her if it's real because it wouldn't be very polite.

"What?" she shouts again, but this time I'm not saying anything. Auntie Clare is hard of hearing.

I can feel the blood rushing up to my face, and across the room I can see Frank spying on me through the bottom of his Chivas glass. In the glass, his face is gross and distorted and his teeth appear closer together.

"Is this fox?" I say loudly because everyone's listening by

now anyway.

My auntie says, "Yes," and tweaks the fox on its petrified nose as my mother brushes past me and barks, "Don't be dense, Diane. Of course it's goddamned fox!" I duck back behind my auntie and continue circulating the pigs-in-a-blanket because I don't want Frank to meet my mother right now, or notice the family resemblance.

Across the room, Uncle Lenny works the crowd. On our way in, my brother called him the same cheap hustler he'd always been. "Remember Vegas?" Wayne asked. I nodded. Once Uncle Lenny flew us all to Las Vegas to visit him and gave us the royal treatment; we toured ghost towns and chased tumbleweed.

When I pass the table with the Chivas on it, I splash a little more into my glass. Gram sidles up close to me, holding out her own glass. "Be a dear," she says. I hold out the Chivas bottle for her but when I look at the glass, I notice a hairline crack that starts on the edge and continues down the side of it. A trickle of blood slowly slides off my grandmother's lip.

"Gram." I reach out and wipe the corner of her mouth with a cocktail napkin that has "Many Happy Returns" emblazoned across it. The other napkins on the table near the Jell-O mold say "Surprise!" but it was no surprise.

I get her a new glass and fill it an inch high with liquid. She smiles at me, swirls the booze around in her glass and says, "That's a dear." She stays quietly beside me, sipping on her drink, until I begin to move away. She yanks on the back of my dress and catches it in one of her rings. The dress tears a little, but not so anyone would notice.

"Yes, Gram?" I turn and look at her. Her spectacled eyes are fixed on someone on the other side of the room. I carefully follow her gaze. They're fixed on Frank. I look away.

She points at him with a shaky finger and says, "That man is no friend of your father's." And then she begins making her way across the carpet, squeezing through the crowd of people now assembled in her living room.

I'm not sure what to do, so I move toward the kitchen to refill a tray. Uncle Lenny turns a highball glass upside down on the coffee table, trapping cubes. "It's a safe bet," he says to Jean-Pierre.

In the kitchen, my mother is whispering softly into the ear of a salesman I do not recognize.

"What exactly are you doing?" she says to me. The man doesn't look up from my mother's neck.

"I'm filling up." I gesture to the sterling silver tray commemorating twenty-five years of marriage between my grandmother and grandfather. I throw on a few cheese twists because I don't see the pigs-in-a-blanket, and because I suddenly feel as if I have to justify my being in my grandmother's kitchen there with them.

"I know what you've been up to," she says quietly, and then she and the salesman I don't know file past me and into the living room.

I drag a chair across the linoleum floor, and sit down next to a half-empty bottle of Chivas and a tray of sandwiches shaped like little hearts.

✧

We Could Stay Here All Night

I met Frank on a wide-bodied 747 on the flight from Vancouver to Montreal. He had a nice face and even teeth. Forty thousand feet above sea-level, we said hello, ordered a few of those miniature airline drinks, and played a hand of gin rummy. We watched a bit of "Blame it on Rio" until we couldn't stand it anymore, and then ordered a few more of those mini drinks on account of they were so mini.

On our way to the baggage carousel we did it in a broom closet with "Do Not Enter" on the door. It was smelly and hot, but not totally without romance. And it was quiet; quieter than I'd remembered it being in a long long time. After it was over, and Frank and I were still waiting for our luggage to come down, he asked me if everything was all right. I couldn't remember anyone ever asking me that before, so I said yes, it was okay.

Outside the terminal while Frank hiked out to long-term parking to hunt for his car, I waited at the curb next to our luggage in the pouring rain. Frank's bags were plaid and matched. I'd brought a single suitcase of black clothing, all I had. Then Frank pulled up next to the curb, cut off a taxi, and honked.

As we headed south towards the city, Frank told me a little more about himself. I listened, but after a while it was as if he was talking just to hear himself talk. When he cut the engine in front of my mother's house, I opened my eyes. "Do you want me to come in?" he asked.

I shook my head and stepped into the middle of the dead end street. I watched Frank pull away from the curb and, for a moment, he reminded me of someone I once knew. Then I turned and walked toward the house. My heels clicked across the pavement. Upstairs, a window opened and my mother thrust her head out. "Diane? Is that you?" she called. Her voice sliced through the silence of the neighbourhood and made the new dog bark.

I looked up. She was wearing something strapless so that from where I was standing she looked naked.

Frank and I didn't see much of each other in the days before the funeral, at least not like we saw each other in the broom closet at Dorval airport, but we did bump into each other a few days later on St. Lawrence Boulevard. I was coming back from the market with my friend Patty, who'd insisted on buying a live chicken for dinner and strangling it herself, when I spotted him. He was walking along the street with a woman my age.

"Shit," I said. "That's him."

"Who?" Patty said.

"The guy from the plane, the guy from the closet," I said, but I wasn't sure why.

"Which guy?" But the expression on my face must have told her which guy because she simply smiled and said, "So." Then she grabbed me and kissed me full on the mouth, hoping he'd sort of walk on by, without a second glance. I knew what she was doing because we'd done it before. So there we were, in the middle of the east end, necking like crazy, when Frank said, "Hello again," like it was a line from a love song.

I grinned and tried wiping Patty's lipstick away.

"I'm sorry, we haven't met," Patty said, linking arms with me. "Are you a friend of Diane's, too?" I wanted to kill her for the extra emphasis she'd put on the word "too" because nothing was going on and for some reason I wanted Frank to know that.

"A friend of Diane's," he repeated, for whatever reason.

"Frank, Patty. Patty, Frank." I waved my hand back and forth between the two of them, then gave up with the lipstick.

That's when I glanced at the woman beside Frank. She had the exact same niceness about her face and evenness about her teeth that Frank had.

"This is Leslie," he said. Then added, "My daughter," but he didn't have to.

Frank introduced me to his daughter as an old friend from Montreal, but neither of us bothered introducing his daughter to Patty. Frank was cool. He didn't even flinch at the thought of me and Patty standing there kissing, a chicken squawking in a gunnysack pressed between us.

When we were just about to leave, Frank reached out and squeezed my hand. It was a warm and friendly squeeze that told me he remembered about the broom closet. His daughter watched us wordlessly, and it occurred to me then that she was probably a very good daughter. Then he said, "I'll call," and they were gone.

"So," Patty said again. Then we went back to her place and she strangled the chicken while I grew morbid and threw up.

In the kitchen, I sit there slurping Chivas and imagine my grandmother slipping stealthily through the crowd to where Frank's sitting. But Frank doesn't get up, he just keeps sitting there holding onto his drink while my grandmother's eyes pierce holes through him. Then this very bright light starts shining through the holes. And when he opens his mouth, I hear him saying, "Yes, Gram," and I don't know why *he's* calling *her* Gram. "I did it in the broom closet, and I did it in the funeral parlour, and I'll do it here." And then all the blood circulating in my grandmother's body starts to drain out of that damned cut in her lip and there are not enough cocktail napkins to clean it all up.

And while I'm sitting there, I also try to imagine the words "do it" come out of Frank's mouth, but I can't. He wouldn't say something like that; I would. So I rest easy for a bit knowing that it's just my imagination, and maybe there's no Frank after all. No Frank, no fucking, no funeral. But then Auntie Clare comes into the kitchen still wearing the fox around her neck and I know it's real. The fox's fur is matted and sticky and smells suspiciously like Chivas.

"Diane!" she yells, holding onto the fox. Pieces of fur float in the air around her and stick to her hands. I know she wants me to talk to her, but I'm not sure I can. Besides, I suddenly feel reluctant to leave my spot by the sandwiches and the Chivas even for a moment. But then she starts yelling again and I begin whispering to her not to worry because everything is going to be all right after all.

We Could Stay Here All Night

I pull fox hair from her face and hands. It upsets my auntie quite a bit that the fox seems to be shedding. She opens and closes her mouth furiously.

"I knew that man wasn't a friend of your father's," my grandmother says, swinging into her kitchen. "I simply knew it." She says "knew" but it comes out sounding like "canoe."

"Diane," my grandmother says softly. "Why didn't you tell me?"

When the phone call about my father I'd been expecting my whole life finally came, I was at Vancouver's Pacific National Exhibit. I was making my hair stand on end in the Science Center, eating pink cotton candy, and laughing and laughing and laughing. Frank and the broom closet were still days in the future.

By the time I finally got back to my apartment on Fourth Avenue, the little red light on my answering machine was flashing. I pushed the play button, but I didn't have to. It was my brother's recorded voice saying, "Diane." He paused for a while, then said, "I hate these fucking things." Then the line went dead and stayed dead for a very long time.